A Local French Affair

An accusation divides a village

Graham Bishop

Also by the same author

Joker in the Pack

Commissaire Pierre Rousseau mysteries:

Achilles' Helmet

The Athenian Connection

The Crusader's Chronicle

Return to the Parthenon

The Walking Man

(in French)

Le Grand Mystère de Gornac

For Madame Georgette Lafosse who welcomed us to the village and showed us so much friendship and kindness when we arrived over 30 years ago.

And for my wife who loved the house and the village as much as her family does still.

Preface

I wrote the original version of this story in French inspired by conversations with a neighbour about her life between the two World Wars in the small villages of Gornac and Gonin in the south-west of France. She told me of the injustice done to a servant girl wrongly accused of theft.

When I was invited to present the original novel to an audience in the local library a further mystery was revealed. No-one had ever heard of the story, which would undoubtedly have caused much discussion in a small village at the time and been passed down.

When expanding the story into a novel I made frequent use of the history of the two villages published by The Association ASPECT in 2015, in order to evoke the atmosphere of the Twenties in which the events took place. I am grateful for their research.

Graham Bishop
June 2nd 2019

Main Characters:

Dr Paul Lasserre, born 1898, GP in Gornac, 26 years old in 1924. 1927 meets **Jacinthe Lévesque.** In 1932 he leaves the village for Bordeaux and marries Jacinthe.

The Bourdet family:

Antoine Bourdet, veteran of WWI and miller, born 1882. Died in 1927 aged 45. Called up to the army in August 1914, returned wounded in 1918. Died in 1927.

Louise Bourdet, his wife, born 1885, died in 1920 of 'Spanish Flu'.

Marie Bourdet, their daughter, born 1905. Lost her mother at 15. Married at 23 in 1928 to Alain Duvigneau.

The Beynard family :

Élise Beynard, born 1876. Died in 1927. Married Gustave Coustaut in February 1914, aged 38.

Gustave Coustaut born 1882, veteran of WWI. Married Élise Beynard in February 1914 aged 32. Called up in August 1914. Returned from the war, wounded, in 1918. Died 1924.

Léonce Beynard, solicitor/notary, born 1878. Married **Agnès,** in 1880. Called up August 1914. Taken prisoner in 1917. Returned in 1919.

Lucette Beynard, born 1885. Married Albert Marceau in 1905. Widowed 1917. A son, **Francis,** born 1906.

Grandmother Beynard died 1895. Their mother died in 1906.

The Marceau family:

Albert Marceau, born 1882. Married Lucette Beynard in 1905. Called up August 1914. Killed 1917.

Francis Marceau, their son, wine broker, born 1906. Married **Eugénie** in December 1927.

Their daughter, **Odette,** born 20th November 1928.

The Duvigneau family :

Bernard and **Simone Duvigneau**, family of wine-makers. Three sons : **Jean-Luc, Jean-Bernard** and **Alain.** Two daughters : **Simonette** and **Marguerite**.

Alain their youngest son, born 1905. Married Marie Bourdet Easter 1928.

The Tremblay family :

André Tremblay, 62, Bernard Duvigneau's uncle. Emigrated to Québec about 1890. Owner of a pulp mill near to Chicoutimi. **Louise,** 56, his wife.

Jacques, 33 and **Pierrette** 31

Étienne and **Thérèse,** 28, twins

Daughters-in-law **Marguerite,** married to Jacques and

Anne, married to Étienne.

Gornac, **France, 1927**

Prologue

Monday, 19th September 1927

Marie Bourdet burst into the main room of the house she shared with her father desperately looking for him, but Antoine Bourdet was still at work in his windmill. She sank exhaustedly onto a chair to recover from the fright and the panic which was overwhelming her. Later she roused herself and took a long drink of water from the well bucket.

Leaving the house she made her way along the track to the windmill. Inside, her father was busy sorting his sacks of flour. He started on seeing his daughter enter.

"What on earth are you doing here, Marie? Why aren't you at work helping Madame Coustaut's family after her funeral? Have they sent you home?"

Realising she was about to faint, Antoine caught her before she could fall and made her sit on the bench. He sat beside her and put his arms round her.

"Tell me, my dear. What's happened, Marie? Has someone attacked you?"

"No papa, nothing like that. Oh papa! I'm not a thief. I've never taken anything from Madame Coustaut's house, I promise you."

"But of course you haven't! Calm yourself! Who's called you a thief?"

"Madame Coustaut's brother, Léonce. He and his wife and sister have been searching the house for the family jewels they say Madame Coustaut must have hidden somewhere. When they couldn't find them Léonce accused me of having stolen them. It's not true, papa, I swear. I've never seen any jewels in the house. I didn't even know Madame had any. I've never been in her bedroom. She didn't allow it. It's not my fault if they can't find them. They must still be somewhere in the house. Papa, I'm not a thief … "

"Of course not, my dear. There's been a misunderstanding. He was just frustrated and angry I expect. When the jewels turn up he'll apologise, I'm sure."

"You don't know him like I do, papa. He'll never apologise. Even if they do find the jewels, he'll never say sorry."

"Don't upset yourself, my dear. Go back to the house. I've nearly finished here and then I'll come home. I'll go and see his sister Lucette. We go back a long way and I'm sure she doesn't think you're a thief."

"Thank you, papa. I love you."

Marie left the windmill and sought the safety of their house.

1924

Chapter 1

Tuesday, February 26th 1924

Late that afternoon Madame Coustaut's maid, Marie Bourdet, climbed the spiral staircase leading to the front door of an imposing house on the outskirts of the village and knocked timidly. There was no response. She knocked a second time, more loudly this time. Still no response. Banging her fists on the door, more out of panic than hope, she realised the doctor was not there.

'Perhaps he is with a patient in the village or even in another village outside Gornac.'

Fear rising from the pit of her stomach, she dared not return to her choleric and hypochondriac mistress without being able to assure her she had informed the doctor she required him to attend to her immediately.

She went back down the staircase looking back several times in the hope the doctor would appear in the doorway as if by a miracle. But, glancing back in vain one last time from the bottom of the steps, she set off down the road which led to the centre of the main village.

'I'll try first in the Grand Hôtel on the market square.'

Normally she would not have the courage to enter such a grand place to ask for him. Hotels like that were were not for the likes of her.

Darkness was falling and without the soft rays from the winter sun to keep her warm, she shivered. She could not afford to buy herself a proper coat on her meagre wages. She was only wearing her thin maid's uniform over which she has pulled a well-worn cardigan, her one luxury.

"I'll just have to walk quickly to keep myself warm," she said out loud.

In the distance she could see the electric street lamps lighting up the main village. In the square in the nearby hamlet of Gonin outside the house where she and her father lived, there was also a street lamp, installed less than two years before. At the time she marvelled at this miracle of lighting which even made the stars disappear it was so bright. With time, she missed the stars.

'It must be like that in the big cities. There are surely lots of street lights in Bordeaux. One day I'll go to see them.'

She hurried on towards the village. The road itself was not well lit and she tripped several times over the many potholes in the badly maintained surface. In the fields by the side of the road she could hear, but not see, the cows grazing noisily or chewing the cud they had consumed earlier. She shivered on hearing mice, or more probably rats, which she had a horror of, running along the ditches on both sides of the track.

She passed by the new communal wash-house which had been built only a year before and further on by the saw-mill belonging to two brothers. At last she arrived at the first house in the village on the right, where one of the brothers lived and carried on his business as a smith, carter and carriage maker. In the other half of the house his sister-in-law ran a grocery and millinery shop.

A little further on she paused for a moment in front of what remained of the Hôtel du Commerce after the great fire ten years before. It had been a dramatic event in her life. She was only nine when it happened and was something she would never forget. From their house by the windmills her family had heard the sound of the fire and the sharp crack of the roof beams as they exploded. They had looked out and seen smoke rising in an enormous grey column high into the sky lighting up the whole area. From all over the village people had run out of their houses to watch the disaster happening in front of their eyes, knowing there was nothing they could do to save the hotel.

The building had still not been restored and that evening as she walked by the ruins she could still detect the slight smell of burnt bricks and wood.

But she did not linger. She was in a hurry. She ran past the Post Office, newly built and a huge event in the life of the village, and at last reached the market square in front of the Mairie. There she hesitated. The Grand Hôtel, stood proudly facing the square behind its impressive iron railings and entrance gates. The square itself was lit by the three street lamps which the mayor had only recently had installed.

'It's like daylight here,' she thought, as she stared across at the hotel.

She could see through the windows on the ground floor and make out people moving about inside; important people who are chatting, drinking and dining at tables laid with white cloths, a world d of luxury almost unimaginable to the young woman. A world she dreamt of entering one day, but which remained unobtainable in her present circumstances.

'One day I promise I'll eat there myself …. '

As she watched a man came out of the hotel and looked across to where she was standing unable to move in the middle of the square.

"What on earth are you doing out there, Marie?" Dr Paul Lasserre called across. "What are you waiting for? It's cold and you aren't wearing a coat. Come on! Come inside."

She walked forward hesitantly towards the voice of the doctor who remained standing in the doorway of the hotel a black silhouette against the light from the inside. Finally she recognised him.

"Monsieur le docteur! It's you I've come to find. My mistress …"

"Your mistress can wait. Come inside quickly. You're shivering, young lady."

"But Monsieur le docteur, Madame is suffering from a bad stomach, her liver. It's urgent," Marie objected, partly for the sake of form but mostly out of fear.

"Don't worry, Marie. I'll tell her I was at Castelande and that you walked all the way there to find me. So we have a good hour before we have to go and see her. Come inside. You need to warm up by the fire."

"But ..."

"Come on, that's enough! You know as well as I do, Marie Bourdet, that it's nothing serious, but if your mistress wants to keep paying me for visits and for giving her medicines, then so be it. But I'll go when it suits me."

The blunt words of the doctor, which Marie knew to be true, helped her overcome her hesitation. She followed the doctor into the main room of the hotel where he made her sit by the roaring wood fire in the grate whilst he fetched a mulled wine for her and an Armagnac for him. When he returned he handed the *vin chaud* to Marie and sat down in a comfortable armchair opposite her.

Marie perched stiffly on the edge of her seat uncomfortable in the smart surroundings of the hotel.

"Relax! Madame Coustaut can't see you here. Tell me a bit about what you do at the Coustaut house, Marie. You have grown into a pretty young woman and must have dreams, ambitions for the future? Do you have a boy friend? Talk to me. I can help you."

Marie looked at him with a mixture of embarrassment and excitement. This was the first time she had found herself talking to an adult who was treating her as an adult.

'But am I really an adult yet?'

Normally her conversations with Madame Coustaut – if that was the right description for the verbal exchanges they had – consisted mostly of orders on the part of her mistress and assent on her part. She never dared to say no, it was not her place.

But the doctor had asked her serious questions and she needed to think of answers. Even with her father such a conversation was rare. She sat up straighter in her chair, swallowed some wine too quickly, spluttered and started again more slowly.

"I've been working for Madame Coustaut for three years. I started the year before you came to the village. I have to arrive at six in the morning to prepare breakfast for Monsieur Coustaut before he goes to work for Monsieur Serizier in the windmill next to my father's."

"Does Coustaut behave correctly towards you, Marie?" asked Lasserre, who had noticed on his visits to the house the way the former soldier looked at the young woman.

She hesitated before replying.

"He does often touch me – on the arm, on the shoulder or on my back. That's all."

"Really? That's all he does?"

"He makes me feel nervous when he's there and it's unpleasant, but I think he's too afraid of Madame to try anything else." And quickly she added: "But I beg you, please don't say anything about that to my father, Monsieur le docteur."

"Calm yourself. Don't worry, I promise I won't say a word. After he has gone to work what do you do?"

"I clear the table of the remains of their evening meal. I do the washing up and put everything away. Then I start to clean the house.

"Madame Coustaut comes down at about eight o'clock and I prepare her breakfast. She automatically criticizes everything I have done since I arrived that morning and usually I have to do it all again. I admit there are times when I don't do much before she comes down because I know I'll have to redo it!"

"Well done! But she's a difficult woman, so be careful, Marie."

"I am careful, Monsieur le docteur, but it is hard at times not to react. I can't afford to lose the job – for my father's sake too."

He waited as she paused.

"Then she gives me a list of the things she wants me to buy here in the village or at the Caïffa store in Gonin. Normally I have to do the shopping and get lunch ready for midday. She gives me the exact money for the shopping and demands a receipt for everything."

"Does Monsieur Coustaut come back at midday?"

"Usually, yes."

"Do you eat with them?"

"Oh no! I eat afterwards if they leave me anything. If not, I go home quickly to get something to eat if I can, but often Madame doesn't allow me to go."

"So you won't have eaten anything since you left your house at six in the morning?"

"No."

She shrugged her shoulders.

"I'm used to it."

Paul Lasserre fell silent, lost in thought.

'How can this sort of situation still exist in 1924?' After all that women did during the Grande Guerre while the men were away, how is it they are still treated as second class citizens? And so often by women themselves.

'As for Gustave Coustaut, he suffered terrible conditions in the trenches and still has shell fragments in his body. I can hear the effects of the gas on his breathing too. I'm not excusing his behaviour, it's just a fact.'

He turned back to Marie who was drinking her mulled wine more cautiously this time, taking small sips, waiting anxiously for Lasserre to speak, wondering if she had said too much.

"Tell me about the rest of your day at the Coustauts'. Do you have time off? Sundays?"

Marie shrugged her shoulders and looked at him without understanding.

"I do what Madame tells me to do. I wash up, I go to the wash-house to wash the clothes. Monsieur Coustaut's work clothes always need washing as they're usually covered in flour from the mill. I go shopping and then I prepare their evening meal."

"You work until what time?"

"Until Monsieur and Madame go to bed. Around eight o'clock in the winter, later in the summer."

"And then you go home?"

"Of course! Where else would I go at that hour? Oh! I'm sorry, Monsieur le docteur, I didn't mean to be rude!" she stammered.

"Don't worry, Marie. It was a silly question."

He held her gaze for a few moments, which embarrassed her and she lowered her eyes.

"Can you tell me what you earn?"

"No. My father receives my wages. It's what he arranged with Madame Coustaut. Father gives me some pocket money when he can, but we are poor, Monsieur le docteur. It's a real effort for father to work and mill work is hard. He suffered terribly during the war. He still has nightmares and I often hear him cry out at night. He's no longer the father I loved when I was little. He's exhausted. That cursed war!"

She paused for a moment.

"We live alone since my poor mother died four years ago when I was fifteen. She died of the Spanish 'flu like so many others," she said, bursting into tears and sinking back into her chair.

Lasserre did not react. He knew that what she described was not unusual in the village. The War Memorial was not erected until three years after the end of the war when they were sure everyone who could return had returned. Thirteen names were engraved on the memorial, thirteen men of Gornac. Thirteen broken families.

But war memorials do not show the names of the broken men who do come back. For them finding work is difficult. Nobody wants to take on these former soldiers, prematurely old, who return with their injuries and their nightmarish memories.

For young men after a war in which they were too young to fight there is plenty of work. The big vineyards are always short of workers particularly at harvest time when strong young men arrive from all over Europe and the owners of the vineyards set up camps to house and feed them.

'For young girls their only choice is to work as a maid or to get married – which may amount to much the same thing,' he admitted to himself.

Marie had recovered from her fit of sobbing and Lasserre took her hand.

"Right. It's time to go and see your mistress. Don't worry. Everything you have told me will stay between us. Let's get in the motorcar."

He strides out of the hotel followed by Marie. His vehicle is parked on the market square near to the village pump. Lasserre is proud of his 1922 5 CV Citröen, a present to himself to celebrate the end of his medical studies in Bordeaux. The villagers were in total awe of it when he first drove into the village. His was the first car many had seen.

Standing by the motorcar, Marie hesitated, taken aback by seeing it up so close for the first time. Under the lights of the square the black shell of the vehicle gleamed like the skin of a mysterious powerful animal. She watched fascinated as the doctor went to the front of the car and turned a handle sticking out of the bonnet.

She jumped back in fright as the roar of the engine suddenly broke into the silence of the evening, reverberating off the walls of the surrounding buildings in the square. The beast bellowed like a bull before settling back to purr like a cat a few seconds later.

"What are you waiting for, Marie? Come and sit beside me. She doesn't bite," said Lasserre, stowing the handle away and climbing up onto his seat.

The young woman walked round the vehicle to the other side. It was an effort to heave herself up onto the shiny green leather bench-seat.

"Is this your first time in a motorcar?" he asked with a smile. "You'll see. She will appear to be going very fast, but here in the village I take care because the mayor has set a speed limit of twelve kilometres an hour. No doubt when he has his own motorcar he'll increase it!"

The short journey between the Gornac and the hamlet of Gonin lasted a only few minutes but for Marie it was like a ride straight out of one of the stories her mother used to read to her from The Arabian Nights when she was little. She gripped the side of the car tightly, feeling dizzy, not because of the mulled wine, but because she had the impression of being on a magic carpet flying at tremendous speed over the village promising her everything she ever dreamt of at night as she lay alone in her bed.

They arrived in Gonin all too quickly and drove past the three windmills with their enormous sails reaching out like supplicant arms silhouetted darkly and menacingly against the low light from the half moon. Immediately afterwards the motorcar stopped outside Marie's house.

"There. Now go straight home, Marie."

"But, Monsieur le docteur ... "

"Don't worry. I'll tell Madame Coustaut you were very brave to come and find me on foot so far in the dark. Otherwise I wouldn't have come this evening to see her. And that I dropped you off at your house on the way because you were exhausted."

He jumped down from the driving seat and went round to the other side to help her step to the ground. He waited to see her safely inside the house and climbed back up behind the wheel to do the hundred metres to the Coustaut house. Grabbing his medical bag off the back seat he went up to the front door, knocked and waited.

Gustave Coustaut opened the door to him.

"Monsieur le docteur! Thank you for coming. My wife is very ill. Come in, come in, please."

The veteran of the Grande Guerre invited Lasserre to follow him. He shuffled along the corridor dragging his left foot, a souvenir of the battle of the Somme.

Lasserre stopped him for a moment:

"How are you, Gustave? How is your breathing?"

Coustaut turned away without a word and opened the door of the living room.

Élise Coustaut was sitting in an armchair near the fire. It was hot in the room and Lasserre immediately took off his coat.

"Good evening, doctor. I'm so pleased to see you. I'm not well, as you can see," she said, simpering.

Suddenly springing up out of her chair, and without waiting for his reply, she burst out:

"But where is that lazy good for nothing girl? Isn't she with you, doctor? Where is she?"

"Good evening, Madame Coustaut," he replied. "I dropped Marie off at home on my way here to see you ..."

"..."

"... because she's exhausted after having walked all the way in the dark to Castelande to find me. She told me she hadn't eaten all day, so I thought she had the right to go home at this late hour."

"But of course, doctor. You did the right thing. The poor girl, she must have been hungry. She's a real treasure, you know. I tell her that every day. I don't know what I'd do without her, what with my husband not being in the best of health."

She sat down again forgetting to invite the doctor to do the same.

"It's a scandal, doctor. Gustave is a hero of the Somme and what does the country do for him? Nothing! It's shameful. He has even had to accept work at Monsieur Serizier's windmill, he who was a master wheelwright before the war. My husband a mere mill worker after all he went through in the trenches! Monsieur Serizier is a kind man, but I repeat, it's shameful."

"Calm yourself, Madame Coustaut. You are right, but often life is not fair. The war is over and we have to adapt. You are lucky to still live in this beautiful house and at least you still have your husband. May I remind you that in the village there are many widows and children with no father."

"You are so right, doctor. Those poor little children. I do still have my dear Gustave."

Suddenly noticing he was in the room, she barked:

"Gustave! Don't just stand there dreaming. Go and fetch a glass of wine for the doctor."

"That's not necessary."

He indicated to Coustaut to stay put.

"So, Madame Coustaut, what exactly is wrong?"

Chapter 2

Wednesday, February 27th 1924

Marie awoke as usual at half past five the following morning. The cockerel in the field near the house was noisily welcoming the new day but she was so used to him she no longer heard his crowing. She remained in bed for a few minutes thinking about the events of the previous evening. The memory of her ride sitting beside the doctor in his magical motorcar caused her to smile, but straight away she remembered she had to go to work and that Madame was sure to scold her and reprimand her in that rasping snappy voice of hers.

This brief glimpse of a more luxurious way of life disconcerted her and it took a great effort of will for her to leave the warm and protection of her bed. She dressed quickly, went down the ladder from the mezzanine over the main room where she slept and prepared breakfast for herself and her father.

The remains of the fire in the hearth still giving out some warmth from the night before. She stirred the embers and added some kindling and a log to get it going again so she could heat the water for coffee.

Her father's bedroom door opened. He came into the room. kissed her good morning on both cheeks and gratefully took the bowl she held out to him.

"How's the work going at the mill, papa?"

"Not well, my dear," he relied, sipping hos coffee. "Old windmills have had their day. After four hundred years of honest work they're almost finished, worn out. I don't know if I can keep going much longer. Industrial milling like they do now in Cadillac will finally put me out of business.

"Don't say that, papa. People still appreciate the old methods and the quality of your flour."

"Perhaps, my dear. But since the war people aren't earning so much and it's difficult for older people to find work in the countryside. In the end it's all a question of money. I can't produce my flour at the price the modern mills can. And you know well I'm not as strong as I was. The work is hard and I'm not a young man any more."

Marie hated to see her father so tired and discouraged, but she knew he was right. Modernisation of the milling industry and the lower prices it brought would lead inevitably to the closure of their windmill and the others in the village. The disappointment and lack of work would kill her father she was sure.

"But be quick, my girl. You'll be late," he said, kissing her again and pushing her towards the door.

It was still dark at that hour despite the street lamp on the square. She shivered in the low morning temperature which her cardigan did nothing to soften. Madame Coustaut's house was not far down the road. She hurried across the little square, passed the Au Caïffa grocery store and crossed the road to reach the front door. As usual the door was not locked and she let herself in. Her first task was to rekindle the fire in the kitchen and to prepare breakfast for Monsieur Coustaut.

The table in the dining room was still covered with the remains of the meal of the evening before. She needed to heat some water so she could do the washing up and put everything away before Madame got up. But she would do that after Monsieur had left for work.

The water started to boil in the pot suspended over the fire. She prepared his coffee and put some bread on the small table in front of the hearth. Sometimes she dared eat a little herself, but that morning it was too late. She could hear him coming down the stairs.

Coustaut limped into the room. Marie knew that in the morning the injury to his leg always felt worse and his mood would be as bad as the pain he experienced.

"Good morning, Monsieur Coustaut," she said politely, knowing he would not reply as he went across to his usual chair. He sat down heavily and picked up a piece of bread to dunk it in his bowl of coffee. Marie turned away and busied herself clearing the dining table uncomfortably conscious that Coustaut's eyes would be on her back watching her movements. Still he said nothing.

She finished clearing the plates and dishes and carried everything into the kitchen. When she returned she faced him and asked:

"Would you like another coffee, Monsieur Coustaut?"

Unable to hold her gaze, he lowered his eyes as he replied:

"No! You know perfectly well I don't have time. I have to get to the windmill. Why do you always ask me the same question every morning? Just to annoy me? You're a useless girl, just like my wife says."

Marie did not react to his insults. She was used to this routine every morning. Finally he stood up and went out without a word. She watched him go and breathed a sigh of relief, but nonetheless she felt some sympathy for this grouchy old soldier who she knew felt embittered at having to work as a simple labourer after having been a skilled craftsman before the war.

*

Gustave Coustaut made his way slowly up the track towards the three windmills silhouetted on their mounds against the sky dominating the hamlet. The first of the three mills had been built in the 1580s about ten years later than the mill called Cazault on the hill above Gornac itself. The other two there in Gonin and a fourth called Sterlin across the fields towards the main village had followed in the seventeenth century according to local tradition. With five windmills between them Gornac and Gonin had become an important centre for making flour. But all that was about to change.

'*What on earth will I do when Serizier and Bourdet close their mills as surely they soon will,*' he wondered. '*Sitting at home with Élise wife badgering me all day will be the death of me.*'

He knew there were still some faithful customers, but they came less and less frequently to buy their flour direct from the mills. The flour coming from Cadillac, which was now sold in the grocery stores here and in the village, was cheaper and finer. The new systems used steel grinding rollers and so the milling was smoother and of more consistent quality. Coustaut feared that soon the sails on the windmills in Gonin, in Gornac and in many other villages around would soon no longer turn in the wind.

Full of such thoughts he entered the mill to start work.

*

Marie was busying herself with the housework when Madame Coustaut came into the kitchen an hour later.

"So, my girl, what airs you are putting on now! Riding in the doctor's motorcar; going home without my permission and here you are this morning as if it was nothing out of the ordinary!"

"I'm sorry, madame, but the doctor insisted I come with him in the motorcar. I didn't know he was going to send me home before he came to see you."

"You should have refused, my girl! Didn't you want to know if I was feeling better or even if I was still alive? Really, it's too bad! You're lucky the doctor gave me some excellent pills last night and that I'm feeling better already. But now you must go immediately to the pharmacy with this prescription."

"But, madame, I haven't finished the housework yet and ..."

"Contradict me one more time and I'll dismiss you. Go! Now!"

"You don't want me to prepare your breakfast first, madame?"

"Stubborn as a mule as usual, Marie! Go! This minute! I must have those pills. If you carry on like this I'll be dead before you return, you wicked girl."

She moved towards Marie, her hand raised in anger. The young woman ran across the room to the door, where in the doorway she turned and hesitated.

"What is it now, girl?"

"The prescription, madame. Without it …. "

Purple with rage Élise Coustaut threw the prescription at Marie who grabbed it off the floor and fled outside.

Leaving the house to go to the pharmacy she passed by the grocery store again. Its strange name – *Au Planteur de Caïffa* – fascinated her. Three times a week the owner, Monsieur Moustié, would send his young assistant to go round the village and the nearby farms selling goods from the store. At the beginning it was just coffee which had built the fame of the Caïffa stores, but they soon added a range of spices, yeast and other specialities under the firm's brand.

The genius of the Caïffa brand had been to realise it was vital to go from house to house, and farm to farm to attract a clientele of housewives who lived mostly in isolated rural areas and couldn't easily go to a shop. The handcart, which the agent dragged behind him whatever the weather, was painted in the colours and arms of *Au Planteur du Caïffa* and the man himself wore a bottle green uniform emblazoned with the name of the company. The 'Caïffaman' as he was nicknamed soon became as welcome in the countryside as the postman.

When Marie was a little girl during the Grande Guerre it was an old man who set off on foot between the shafts of the small handcart. Early each morning while still in bed she would recognise the sound of the wheels with their metal rims on the surface of the track outside as he struggled to pull the laden cart along past her house to start his round.

But two years ago to Marie's delight, Alain Duvigneau, the young son of a local winemaker, needing some extra cash, had taken over the round. He used his bicycle to tow the trailer which had replaced the handcart. She woke early on those mornings when he was working to watch him pass by from behind the curtains of the low window by her bed. She prayed that one day he would look up and see her. But he never did. Sometimes she did think she saw a smile cross the lips of the young man as he passed the house. But she couldn't be sure.

Instead of heading straight to the pharmacy in the main village, Marie made a short detour. Reaching the windmills on the hill she saw Monsieur Coustaut working outside the mill on her left. On the other side of the track she knew her father would be busy at this hour inside his windmill greasing the mechanism and cleaning the grind stones. She checked to see if Coustaut was watching her and slipped quickly inside to speak to her father. He looked up as she entered and smiled.

"What are you doing here, my dear? Why aren't you at work?"

"I have to go to the pharmacy for Madame."

"So hurry along! She'll be cross if you delay here."

"I just wanted to give you a hug, *papa*. You looked so tired and down this morning."

"That's very sweet, but don't worry about me. I've plenty of work for a few months yet. But this morning there's hardly any wind and I'll have to turn the sails into what there is. I'll get together with Philippe Serizier to turn the caps of our mills. Poor Gustave will try to help us no doubt, but with his injuries he's no longer strong."

"I could help you," she said.

"No, no! You must run quickly to do your errand. If you're late she'll tear a strip off you."

"She'll do that anyway, papa."

"Away with you, girl. Quickly now," he replied with a smile full of love for his daughter who looked more and more like her mother.

The young woman left the mill and hurried along the track to make up for lost time. She knew her father and Monsieur Serizier would not find it easy to turn the heavy caps using the long tiller bar which reached from the cap down to the mounds each mill was built on. But both men were proud of the way they maintained the mechanisms and the caps would hopefully slide round smoothly on their tracks. If not, they would have to ask the help of the neighbouring farmer with his team of oxen.

*

At the pharmacy Marie had to wait for half an hour as there were so many villagers in the queue. In February it seemed everyone had caught a cold or was feeling depressed. The pharmacist was handing out pills like grapes off a vine at harvest time.

Finally it was her turn. The pharmacist studied the prescription and smiled. He looked at Marie for a second and went into his small laboratory behind the counter. After a short moment he returned and, with a flourish, handed Marie a large bag containing several medicines and pills in a variety of bottles and boxes.

"There, Marie. This is for your mistress. I'll put it on her account."

"Thank you, Monsieur Guichard," she replied, stuffing the bag with some difficulty into her basket.

As she was about to leave she asked:

"Why did you smile when you looked at the prescription, Monsieur Guichard?"

"For me to know, Marie. Don't worry. It's all there."

She left the pharmacy still curious and not satisfied by his reply. She was starting down the track to return to the house when she heard shouts coming from the direction of the windmills. She recognised her father's voice calling for help. She rushed back into the pharmacy.

"Come quickly, Monsieur Guichard. I think there's been an accident at the windmills. I can hear my father shouting for help."

Guichard, accompanied by several customers who were suddenly feeling much better, tumbled out of the shop and ran towards the windmills. Marie got there before the others, having dumped her basket near the doorway of the pharmacy so she could run all the quicker, out of her mind with worry about her father. As she came closer she could see a small group of men and women rushing about at the base of Serizier's windmill. Someone was lying on the ground but it wasn't her father. She saw him send Alain Duvigneau to fetch the doctor from his surgery.

She rushed over.

"Oh! papa! I was so worried you had had an accident," she said, throwing her arms around his neck.

"Calm down, my dear. I'm not hurt, but poor Gustave fell off the mound and I'm worried he's broken his leg."

"But what was he doing up there?"

"He was helping us push the tiller bar so we could turn the cap, but he slipped and fell from the top," he replied, looking at the people who were trying to help the victim and make him more comfortable on the ground. A neighbour placed his jacket over him. The poor man was trembling with cold and shock.

When two men tried to lift him up and carry him towards the Bourdet's house nearby, he screamed so much with pain they almost dropped him and quickly lowered him back onto the ground.

The crowd around him looked at each other making suggestions, not knowing what to do while they waited for the doctor to arrive.

The sound of the engine of the doctor's motorcar made them all look up as it approached. Alain was sitting up beside Lasserre, a big grin on his face, the seriousness of his errand forgotten. The young man jumped off the motorcar at the same time as the doctor landing heavily and almost turning his ankle, which wiped the smile off his face as he winced.

Paul Lasserre approached the injured man, asking those surrounding him to move back so he could attend to the patient. He gently took hold of the man's leg and felt it carefully from the ankle to the hip. Coustaut screamed in agony and passed out.

"We need to carry him back to his house. His leg is broken in two places. Antoine? Do you have a plank or something we could use as a stretcher?"

"Yes, doctor," he replied, heading quickly towards his mill. He returned carrying the narrow top of a table. The men moved forward to lift Coustaut, fortunately for him still unconscious, and place him on the plank. Four of them carried him towards the house.

"Marie! Go and warn Élise. Quickly, before they get there!" said her father.

She ran towards the house, her heart racing in fear of the reaction of her mistress to her news. She banged on the door and opened it with such force that it slammed against the wall behind.

"What on earth do you think you're doing? You don't enter the house like that, Marie! Where are my pills, you wretched girl? I've been waiting an hour at least. You really are impossible ..."

"Madame, it's Monsieur. He ..."

"My Gustave! What's happened to him? Tell me, girl," she shouted, seizing Marie by the shoulders and shaking her, just as the men arrived carrying the makeshift stretcher with the still unconscious Coustaut.

"Gustave! No, no! He's dead! He can't be!" she screamed, and immediately fainted.

Marie tried to catch her but she was too heavy and both of them fell onto the tiles getting in the way of the men who were trying to enter with the injured man. It was Lasserre who restored order. He helped Madame Coustaut to her feet and sat her in a chair. The men couldn't carry Coustaut up the narrow stairs to his bedroom on the first floor, so they put him on the table in the middle of the room.

He was starting to come round but was breathing with difficulty. Lasserre gave him an injection against the pain but Coustaut's eyes suddenly closed and he sank into a coma. Paul looked at him in surprise and examined him more closely.

Opening his shirt he discovered a huge bruise on his side. It was obvious the man had broken several ribs when he fell. A rib must have pierced his lung and he was haemorrhaging internally. The doctor closed his shirt and turned to Madame Coustaut.

"I'm sorry, Madame Coustaut, but your husband is seriously injured. I have done what I can, but ..."

She jumped up from her chair and threw herself over her husband's inert body, cradling his head in her arms.

"He must go to hospital immediately, doctor. What are you waiting for?"

"I fear he's too weak, madame. His wounds are serious and he's bleeding inside. Any movement would kill him."

She sank to her knees in tears beside her husband. Lasserre touched her lightly on the shoulder to console her. Everyone in the room realised Coustaut was dying. They left the room in silence to allow his wife to mourn in peace.

Lasserre looked for Marie but she was leaving in tears with Alain, his arm round her shoulders.

"I'll take her back home," he said, catching the doctor's eye.

Lasserre nodded and was looking for someone who could stay with the poor woman when Antoine Bourdet entered the room. He had gone to fetch Madame Coustaut's sister, Lucette Marceau.

Lucette came in behind him, crossing herself on seeing her brother-in-law lying on the table. She went over to embrace her sister. Lasserre indicated to her to call him when it was over and left the house with Marie's father.

The two men stood outside the front door for a moment.

"Thank you, Antoine, for going to fetch Lucette," he said. "I wasn't sure if the sisters were still speaking to each other."

"Maybe they aren't, but in the circumstances ..."

"Yes, yes. You're right, of course."

"We must let the brother Léonce know. I think he lives in Bordeaux, doesn't he doctor?"

"Yes, he's a notary. I'll telephone him. But watch out, Antoine. I know him a little and I'm certain he'll question you closely to establish the exact cause of the accident. You must speak seriously with Philippe. You must both agree precisely on what happened."

"Thank you, doctor. I will. But, you know, it was one of those stupid little accidents. Any other day Gustave would have picked himself up and laughed at his clumsiness.

"I know, but all the same … "

The two men parted in front of Bourdet's house. Lasserre walked up to the windmills to collect his motorcar and return to his surgery to telephone Léonce Bernard.

Chapter 3

The end of August 1926

Her father left her to sleep in when he went to work at the windmill at seven that morning.

She deserves a long lie-in for once, Bourdet said to himself.

Élise Coustaut had gone to spend a few days with cousins in the Lot and so Marie was on holiday – unpaid of course.

Antoine Bourdet was worried. He knew this season would be his last at the mill. He had agreed with his friend Philippe Serizier that they would shut down their windmills on the same day at the end of September. They simply couldn't carry on. The old ways were no longer viable. They had to face facts. The third windmill on the hill had already stopped turning a year before when Guillaume Bouyre had retired. Work at the windmill called Sterlin on the other side of the road to Saint-Luc-du-Bois had ceased years before. He and Serizier were the last two millers in the village carrying on the age-old tradition.

He covered the few metres between the house and the windmills slowly, as if memorizing every step for the future. Serizier was following the same path. They shook hands in silent greeting and both men entered their mills with a heavy heart.

*

An hour later Alain walked down the track between the windmills. Their sails were turning slowly in the gentle light wind of late August. He could hear the slapping of the canvas against the slats on the four sails and the grinding of the axles rubbing against the cap. Coming from the interior of the windmills he recognised the distinctive sound of the mill-stones turning and grinding the grain.

He stopped for a moment to listen better to these sounds which he had known all his life, but which he was only now beginning to appreciate. He had never known the village without these sounds. Normally he hardly noticed them, they were just background noise. But he realised as he started walking again that over the next few weeks he should listen and savour them as never before. When the sails stopped turning the atmosphere of the village would be changed for ever.

Despite his growing nostalgia that morning he was happy and full of energy. The grape harvest was beginning at last. The Sauvignon Blanc was ready for picking and he had come to invite Marie to help in his father's vineyard. The family's vines extended over about twenty hectares and it would take at least a month depending on the weather to bring the whole harvest in. The journeymen and their families had arrived, but with fifty or so small vineyards in the commune everyone relied on friends and neighbours as well to make up the workforce.

He approached her house and knocked. Marie opened the door immediately as if she had been waiting for him.

"Come in for a minute, Alain. I'm still having breakfast. Do you want a coffee?"

"Sure. Do you know what time it is, Marie? That's some lie-in you've had! But it's good Madame Coustaut is away and you don't have to go to work, because we're harvesting the white grapes today. So, I have come to ask if you would like to work with us in the vineyard?"

"Of course I would! You mean right now, this morning? OK, just wait a second, I'll go and change. I'll only be a minute. Help yourself to coffee."

She rushed up to her room to change, pleased to help with the harvest and overjoyed to be going with Alain. She knew his father was a good man, perhaps a little strict, but kind all the same. The work would be hard but working together with friends and people from the village was always good fun. They would laugh and sing songs together while they worked.

Later, when the grapes were all picked and safely in the winery, the *'pampaillet'* – the harvest supper – would be held to celebrate the end of the harvest. But she nonetheless felt sad because she knew this year would also mark the shutting down of the windmills in Gonin. She was afraid for her father. How would he react to the closure?

She went back down into the main room.

"See, that didn't take long? I'm ready. I'll tell papa where I'm going on the way."

"Let's go then. Work started hours ago, sleepy-head!"

Marie stopped quickly at the windmill and they ran the rest of the way to the Duvigneau family's vineyard, Domaine Le Frègne.

*

Marie helped Alain, his brothers and their father in the vineyard for the rest of the week. Monsieur Duvigneau had hired twenty journeymen to help with the work and so, together with friends and neighbours, they made good progress each day. It was sunny and dry that year of 1926 and later it would be said it was a good vintage.

When Élise Coustaut returned from her holiday in the Lot, Bourdet insisted his daughter be allowed to continue to help with the harvest until it was all in. Knowing the shortage of labour in the village, Madame Coustaut knew better than to refuse.

Marie was over the moon at being able to continue working outside amongst her friends. It was so different from her work inside as a maid for a grumpy old woman.

At first during the picking of the Sauvignon Blanc she was shouted at like everyone else every time she dropped a bunch on the ground, but this happened less and less frequently as she became more skilled. Towards the end of the month they moved on to the red Merlot grapes on the dozen or so rows which were all that was left to do.

Like the other workers she carried a straw basket strapped to her back and learned how to use the curved knife – called locally a *serpette* – to sever the stalks of the bunches of grapes cleanly. Once the basket was full she had to climb up the ladder leaning against the ox-cart and learn how to drop one shoulder and pour all the grapes and the juice into the large vats on the cart. It was not always an easy technique and by the end of the day she always ended up with sticky hair from the grapes which caught in her long dark tresses and the juice which ran down her neck.

Sometimes to give themselves a break from the back-breaking work of picking, Marie and the others took turns at helping to sort the grapes by hand. The rejected bunches lying on the ground were gathered up and spread out on tables. Those grapes that were bruised, rotten or not ripe enough were removed. She also led the oxen pulling the carts laden with the overflowing vats to the winery, urging them on when the slope was steep.

By the end of the day, every muscle in her back, arms and legs ached but she had never felt happier. She walked back with a light heart and opened the door to find her father already finished for the day.

"You look as if you have had a good day my dear."

Antoine Bourdet was tired but happy to see his daughter smiling as she came in.

"Yes, papa. It was lovely to be outside and to work with other people. I often feel so lonely when I am working for Madame and seeing no-one all day."

"I know, my dear. I am sorry you have to work for such a difficult woman, but we need the money."

"We will be alright, papa. One day I'll find a better job and will be able to earn more. Let's forget all that this evening and have supper. I want to tell you all about my day."

*

When everything was gathered in at Domaine Le Frègne, preparations for the harvest supper began as a way of thanking the journeymen and saying good-bye to them as they would be moving on the next day seeking other work.

The meal took place in a large barn on the property. Down the length of the barn in front of the cow and oxen stalls a line of tables was set up. The cows and the oxen looked on fascinated by all this unusual activity before them in their barn.

Alain and Marie took their places side by side.

"Just look at all those bottles down the whole length of the table, Alain! I've never seen so many all at once. Surely we are not going to drink all those?"

"And more," Alain replied with a smile."You'll see. They will all be empty very soon."

The bottles and the loaves of bread placed alongside them formed a low fence between the guests on either side.

Soup was served first. The men took out their personal knives to cut themselves chunks of bread. Once the soup was finished they poured their wine into the warm bowls, as was the local custom, called *chabrol*, and then drank straight from the rim.

"I've never tried that, Alain," she said turning to him. "My mother would never have allowed it and I've never seen papa do that at home."

"Go on then. I dare you," he replied. "It's easy."

Marie poured some wine into her soup bowl and brought it up to her lips.

"Oh! No! " she said, laughing. "Now I've spilt it all down my dress. It's impossible. Anyway, you nudged me!"

"No I didn't," he replied, squeezing her hand. "You're just clumsy!"

The evening became more and more rowdy. The diners tossed the chicken and meat bones onto the floor below the tables, causing fights among the farm dogs waiting impatiently underneath for the scraps to fall. Bottles were emptied and replaced by more. Soon the singing began and an accordionist did his best to accompany them. The evening ended late into the night.

Alain escorted Marie back to her house in Gonin under a starlit heaven.

"Will you be my partner at the harvest ball on Saturday?" he asked.

Marie flung her arms around his neck and kissed him before escaping into the house.

*

That year the celebration and ball to mark the end of the harvest in the commune took place on the hill between the three windmills in Gonin as usual. During the day there was a country market with stalls selling sweetmeats, wine, trinkets and other luxuries. There was even a tombola. An apéritif was served at midday and various games and competitions were organised offering prizes, all accompanied by sound of the local band. The main event was an enthusiastic cycle race around the villages. In the evening the windmills were illuminated, or lighted, as they said at the time. Fireworks were set off as soon as it grew dark. A stray rocket set fire to a straw bale but it was quickly put out when Alain organised a line to bring in buckets of water.

The dancing began after the fire had been extinguished. Alain and Marie were never apart and, like the other young couples, danced till dawn. That Sunday, attendance at mass was sparse.

1927

Chapter 4

Sunday, 18th September 1927

At Bordeaux-Passerelle station Léonce and Agnès Bernard took their seats in the railway carriage to travel to the funeral of his sister Élise Coustaut, who had died of heart-break two days before.

They left the train two hours later at the station in Saint Brice. Their nephew Francis Marceau was waiting for them on the platform in the rain. All three were dressed in black, as were several of the passengers who left the train at the same time and who acknowledged them with a respectful bow of the head as they passed by. Francis embraced his uncle and aunt and took charge of their cases.

Without a further word they left the station and went to his motorcar parked a few metres away. Once they were settled in and the cases stowed Léonce Bernard asked his nephew:

"Is everything ready?"

"Yes, Uncle. The mass begins in the Saint Jean-Baptiste church in Gornac at eleven. The funeral follows and the burial will be in the graveyard in the family tomb. We will place her next to Uncle Gustave."

"And afterwards?"

"At the house, of course. Marie and my mother have arranged everything."

"Gustave's death broke Élise's heart and she never really recovered. I tried to persuade her to come and live with us in Bordeaux, but she didn't want to leave the house."

"Aunt Élise didn't want to be far from my uncle," replied Francis. "She went to mourn by his tomb every Sunday without fail."

"Be honest, Léonce. You invited her to live with us so you could sell the house straight away. You just wanted your share," interrupted his wife.

"Enough, Agnès! Now is not the time," her husband shot back.

Quickly turning back to Francis, he asked:

"And how is your mother? Like me she has lost a sister."

"She's doing alright. As you said Uncle, Aunt Élise never really recovered from Uncle Gustave's death and she became depressed. She only ever went out to go to the church and the graveyard. Recently I had to drive her there as she had become very weak. So her death was not a surprise and the shock is less than it might have been."

"Thank you, Francis, for all you and your mother have done for her. I'm sorry not to have come more often to see her. I'm so busy in the practice."

"Léonce! You didn't come to see her simply because you didn't want to!"

"Be quiet, Agnès, that's enough!"

Embarrassed, Francis looked straight ahead and watched the road. He drove through the village of Coirac and soon entered Gornac. As they drove by the church he said:

"I'm going to take you to the house first. We have plenty of time before the service. Marie will stay in the house during the funeral. I'll then drive us to the church with my mother. The weather is so bad today we have cancelled the funeral procession from the house to the church. The coffin is already there."

He drove through the village and Francis turned left up the track which led between the windmills and to the house in Gonin. Léonce remained silent.

"Thank you, Francis," said his aunt from the back seat. "You've been marvellous and thought of everything. I know it has not been easy for you. How are you? Are you still a wine broker?"

"Yes I am, Aunt. There are lots of winemakers here. The greats like château Cazault, château Espère and château Pouly, but also lots of smaller growers even here in Gonin like Monsieur Lamothe et Madame Couteau, so I have plenty of work, especially now the grape harvest has started."

"That's very good, very good. Your mother says you hope to get married soon … Oh! Here we are already. You must tell me all about it later."

"She opened the motorcar door and went into her late sister-in-law's house without waiting for her husband to accompany her. Inside, Marie was helping Lucette lay the table and put out the food and the glasses.

"Agnès! How lovely to see you," exclaimed Lucette, going over to greet her.

"How are you, Lucette?"

"Oh! Fine, you know. Élise was so ill these last few days it was a release for her. I'm sorry, but the weather is so bad we closed the coffin and it has already been taken to the church."

"Honestly my dear, I prefer it that way. But I know Léonce will be disappointed."

"Somehow I doubt that," Lucette replied, a slight smile playing around her lips.

The door opened and her brother and Francis entered the room. Agnès went over to speak to Marie while Léonce kissed his sister and discussed the arrangements she had made.

"You have done so well, Marie. I know my sister-in-law was not always an easy woman, but she appreciated what you did for her I can assure you."

"Thank you, madame. That's kind. Madame Coustaut was very weak towards the end of her life and Madame Marceau came to help me. Madame never recovered after the accident at the windmill. It was terrible."

"And your father? Is he well?"

"Yes and no. Perhaps you don't know that the windmills are shut down now. It's the end of an era. My father doesn't know what to do with himself."

"That's sad. I loved to see the sails turning in the wind and to hear the grinding of the millstones. That was the beating heart of the village. The atmosphere must have really changed."

"Agnès! Come on! It's time to go to the church."

"We'll continue our conversation later, Marie," she whispered, before turning towards her husband. But Léonce had already left the house. Francis, Lucette and Agnès followed him, thanking Marie with a nod for staying to look after everything.

The door closed and Marie found herself alone in the house. For a moment she felt lost and had no idea what to do. Being alone in this old house where she had witnessed two deaths was painful. What's more this would be the end of her employment after four years of service. The thought scared her, but wasn't this the moment she had been waiting for? The chance to escape from the village and to go to Bordeaux and look for a job.

She was sure Dr Lasserre would help her find lodgings with someone he knew. But how would her father react to her leaving? She was finally an adult and could do what she liked, but she hesitated to abandon her father.

Despite the deeply rooted aversion of country people to sell land or property belonging to the family, Marie knew this was not a house Léonce would wish to keep. She was convinced the brother would want to sell it as quickly as possible. *He's only interested in the money.*

As for the sister Lucette, she wasn't so sure. She and her son Francis didn't own the house they lived in down the steep lane leading to the valley with it's well dated 1604, but rented it from Château Espère. She had not been close to her sister Élise, but she hadn't hesitated to help look after her after the accident, coming every day to prepare meals for her. Francis too had done any repairs which needed doing and attended to the garden. Maybe they would want to take it over. Marie could foresee furious arguments between the brother and sister.

Marie picked up the book of condolences on the sideboard and leafed through it. The majority of the inhabitants of Gonin and several from Gornac had come to pay their last respects to Madame Coustaut in her coffin in the bedroom on the first floor, including Monsieur Coiffard from Château Espère and of course the mayor of Gornac. These comings and goings had caused her a lot of work because of the mud falling off the boots of the visitors which none of them removed before climbing the stairs up to the bedroom.

A knock on the door interrupted her thoughts. She got up to open it. It was Alain standing soaked to the skin in the pouring rain.

"What are you doing here, Alain? I can't let you in, I'm supposed to be guarding the house."

"I just came to see if you were alright," he said, stepping back to avoid the drops falling from the tiles above him.

"That's nice of you."

She looked quickly around.

"Come in just for a minute."

She grabbed him by the lapels of his coat and pulled him towards her. She kicked the door shut behind them with her foot, threw her arms around him and kissed him firmly on the lips.

"There! Now you know how much I love you. No, no! That's enough. Go!" she said, laughing and pushing him towards the door. "You mustn't be seen here. They'll all be coming back from the funeral soon."

Alain left quickly and walked back towards the windmills. He had to step aside as Francis' motorcar went by spattering him with mud.

Marie was frantically wiping up the spots of rain on the floor and on her dress when she heard the motorcar return and voices outside.

Lucette Marceau came in first.

"Is everything all right, Marie?" she asked, noting the spots of rain on the floor and the frightened look on Marie's face. "I saw Alain Duvigneau on the track as we arrived. You didn't let him in did you?"

"For just a moment, Madame Marceau. I'm really sorry."

"Don't worry, I won't say anything. It will be our secret," she whispered as she turned to let the others in.

Agnès and Léonce Bernard entered, followed by their nephew. They stayed near the door to receive the condolences of the villagers who came in and went straight towards the table. They shook the rain off their coats and stamped their feet to remove the mud, before losing no time helping themselves to something to eat and drink.

Marie knew it would take hours to clean up later, but she busied herself serving the guests, with their serious expressions, but who nonetheless did not seem to have lost their appetites.

After a couple of hours the last mourners finally left and the family members flopped down into the chairs, tired and in need of quiet after the emotion of the day. Marie poured them each a glass of wine to restore them.

Léonce was the first one to recover.

"At last it's over! I'm all in. Talking to all these people I hardly know is more than I can take frankly. Where were they when my poor sister needed them?"

"Léonce! You don't know what you're talking about. They were all very generous and helped me to look after Élise. At least they were here … "

"What are you implying, Lucette? That I didn't care for Élise? That I neglected her? That's the last straw! And what did you hope to gain from all the attention you gave her? A bigger share of her will?"

"Uncle! That is completely unjust! My mother did what she did out of the pure goodness of her heart and to suggest otherwise is an insult I can't tolerate, despite the respect I owe you … "

"Enough!" cut in Agnès. "We're all tired and emotional. Léonce, go and fetch my coat. We're leaving for the hotel. On foot," she added. "No need for you to take us, Francis. We all need to calm down. We'll see you tomorrow."

She seized her husband's arm and dragged him to the door under the horrified gaze and crushing silence of the others. They continued staring at the door as it closed.

*

For several minutes nobody moved. Finally, without a word, Lucette began to clear the table and carry the plates and glasses into the kitchen, quickly helped by Marie. Francis sat down with his head in his hands, too upset by what his uncle had said to help them. Eventually he got to his feet and began to tidy up the room.

Everything was finally cleaned and tidied by eight o'clock and the three of them were exhausted. They had hardly spoken a word to each other the whole time.

The scene Léonce had been responsible for had shocked them deeply. Lucette was shattered by the insinuation she was a fortune hunter. It was true she hadn't got on well with her sister for some time – nor with her brother, if truth be told. But recently the two sisters had talked together for hours and Lucette had discovered the reason for her sister's jealousy all those years ago.

She looked at her son and at Marie.

"It's late. Marie, thank you for all you have done this afternoon and evening. You must be exhausted, like us! Go home. Your father must be wondering what has happened to you. Come back tomorrow, but not too early. Around ten o'clock. Is that OK?"

"Of course, Madame Marceau."

She stood up and went to get her coat. As she put it on she turned back to Francis and Lucette.

"Till tomorrow then. Thank you for not saying anything, Madame Marceau."

She opened the door and went out shutting it behind her.

"For not saying what?" asked Francis, intrigued.

"Nothing important. She let her boyfriend Alain Duvigneau in for a moment."

"Better not tell my uncle!"

"Definitely not! He'll imagine all sorts of things. But, Francis, I have things I want to tell you about your Aunt Élise … if you are not too tired."

"Not at all. Go ahead, maman."

"The accusation thrown at me by Léonce about the inheritance made me think. Lots of long buried thoughts came back to me."

"Maman, you don't have to explain anything or apologize. I know … "

"Goodness, I'm not apologizing! I have nothing to apologise for! But I want to tell you about our childhood when the three of us were young and explain why we do not get on well."

"Then it's me who should apologise," he said touching her on the cheek.

"No, no. Move over, I want to sit beside you. There, that's better. Now just listen."

"I'm the youngest in the family as you know. I'm seven years younger than my brother and nine years younger than Élise. And I was our father's pet. I couldn't do anything wrong in his eyes. For Élise, the final straw was that I was much prettier than her … "

"And you're still pretty … "

"Thank you. But where was I … ? Oh, yes. While Élise had to stay in and help our mother with the housework, I used to go out with my friends to play in the fields around the windmills. We were as free as the wind and spent wonderful summers outside.

"There were even spectacular events taking place in the village. I was ten in 1895 when the soldiers came for what at the time were called the Grandes Manœuvres. For us little girls it was marvellous. There were soldiers and horses everywhere. Here in Gonin more than three hundred soldiers and officers were billeted on us."

"But where did they all stay? Three hundred is a lot of men. There aren't enough lodgings today to house so many and no doubt at the time there were even less!"

"No, obviously, but the soldiers didn't have the right to beds. They slept in the barns often beside their horses, or in outhouses and lofts."

"How did they feed all those men?"

"Everything and everyone was requisitioned, especially the bakers. There was an enormous demand for flour and the windmills worked flat out all over the area. They needed three thousand large loaves a day!"

"For three hundred men?"

"No, you silly boy! There were more than three thousand men here all together in Gornac and the surrounding communes. I didn't learn that until later of course. Several of the locals opened cafés and restaurants in the villages. There was lots of activity which was really exciting for us as you can imagine."

"This is all very interesting, maman, but why are you telling me this now?"

"Because, if for us kids it was a great adventure, I think for your aunt Élise it was a real opportunity to find a husband. Of course she was interested in the officers. She was nineteen and there weren't many young men of her age in the village.

"Almost every day there were manoeuvres in the valley between the village and Castelviel on the ridge. The whole population came to watch the spectacle from the hill here. We kids used to run around everywhere and play at soldiers. The officers scrutinised the manoeuvres from viewpoints like here at Gonin from the top windows of the windmills and from the windmill at Cazault on the other side of Gornac. Élise busied herself going round each day offering them sweetmeats and drinks. That was her way of getting to know the officers."

"But it didn't work?"

"No. The poor thing had no success. We even overheard officers talking about her and saying she wasn't pretty enough. It was sad."

She fell silent for a moment and watched the flames flickering in the hearth. Francis waited. He knew she was recalling scenes from when she was a child. Pushing aside the images in her mind, she continued her story.

"The Grandes Manœuvres returned in 1903, but Élise was twenty-seven by then which was considered at the time the age of a spinster. I was eighteen and my parents watched over me very strictly, because of the large number of young men in the area. I was not even allowed to go out this time!"

"You poor thing! So, when did Aunt Élise marry?"

"Wait! So we are in 1903. Our brother had gone to study law in Bordeaux. Élise abandoned all hope of finding a husband and I was even prettier than before. At the dances and harvest balls I danced mostly with Albert Marceau, the son of a winemaker in the village and of course, in order to make him jealous, I left him sometimes to dance with other young men ... "

" ... who were queuing up to have the chance no doubt!"

"You're right. I was in demand! The young men hovered around me, which made my girl friends jealous but not bitterly so, as there there were enough young men in the village at that time to satisfy the expectations of all the young girls. Every one found a boyfriend.

"Élise stood on the side during the dances and didn't get many invitations as all the young men thought she was too old.

"Finally, to cut the story short, Albert and I were married on the 17th June 1905 in the church in Gornac. Léonce was too busy in Bordeaux with his studies, so he said, to come to the wedding, which I was so disappointed about.

"Élise was my maid of honour. She had to watch her younger sister get married before her. That must have been humiliating. Such things were considered important then and perhaps still now. A year later you were born. It was the most marvellous moment in my life and Albert was a fabulous father. He loved you to bits."

She stopped and looked for a moment at Francis, but put up her hand to stop him from speaking.

"I'll tell you more about your father later, but let me finish the story. In February 1914 when she was thirty-eight Élise finally married a carpenter, your uncle Gustave, who was four years younger than her. But on the first of August, so only a few months later, your father and your uncles Gustave and Léonce were recalled to their respective regiments like most of the men in the country when Germany declared war on Russia. Two days later Germany declared war on France.

"Léonce was captured in 1917 and returned from a prisoner of war camp uninjured in 1919. Gustave returned too, but was wounded in body and mind.

"I never saw your father again."

Francis put his arms round his mother and both of them stared into the fire, watching the sparks rising above the flames and disappearing up the broad chimney. They stayed watching the fire until the embers were out.

It was dark when they stood up, retrieved their coats and went out to return home.

*

The front door opened straight into the main room and Marie saw her father dozing in his armchair by the fire. She could smell the soup simmering in the pot over the embers in the slow oven which had been carved into the wall by the fireplace centuries before and she realised she was desperately hungry. She walked softly into the room, took off her coat and went to take a bowl from the sideboard. While helping herself to the soup the ladle touched the side of the bowl and the sound woke her father. He looked at her for a moment without understanding.

"Marie! You're back. That's good. How was it?"

"Wait a minute, papa. I'm so hungry I must eat first."

She sat at the table and swallowed a few spoonfuls of soup. Finally she wiped her mouth with the napkin and looked at her father who was waiting patiently.

"You know, papa, they're not a happy family. The children didn't get on when they were young and the two who remain still don't get on. It's sad."

"Ah! There's a whole story behind that. Mostly jealousy between the two girls and the difference in age, and the fact that Léonce went to Bordeaux to go to university leaving his two sisters and his parents behind in the village."

"I don't like Léonce," she said. "He accused Madame Marceau of looking after her sister just to get a greater inheritance from her. She's not like that, papa, she's really kind and gentle. And she treats me like an equal."

"Yes, I know, my dear. She lost her husband during the war after only nine years together. But that's all past history. You must be tired. Give me a kiss and go to bed."

Marie stood up and approached her father.

"You like her, don't you papa?"

"Who?"

"Madame Marceau, of course."

"Don't be silly. Go to bed."

Marie moved away, but at the foot of the stairs she turned and said:

"If you wanted to marry again, papa, I'd be happy for you."

"Go to sleep," he replied.

*

Léonce and Agnès walked along the muddy track between the windmills to reach the main village. Agnès was furious at her husband's attitude towards his younger sister. She was used to listening to Léonce's snide comments about his family, but normally she preferred to calm things down by not responding. There was no point in having an argument.

"You're right, Agnès, I went too far. I shouldn't have criticised Lucette like that."

Agnès said nothing. They continued along the track, not speaking, to the hotel. The receptionist gave them the key to their room and they went straight up. After changing out of their damp mourning clothes they went down to the dining room. There was a table near the bar. The other diners acknowledged their presence but otherwise left them alone, respecting their mourning.

Paul Lasserre was sitting in his usual place in an armchair by the fire from where he could easily observe their table, while giving the impression he was dozing. Keen observer of body language and good psychologist that he was, he wondered at the reason for the evident irritation between the couple who hardly spoke a word to each other.

He watched them order their meal and choose the wine. He noted it was Agnès who selected the wine and ordered. Léonce seemed to be in a sulk. After the waitress had taken their order, he saw Léonce lean forward and speak quietly to his wife. Paul couldn't hear clearly what he said to her, but everyone in the dining room heard Agnès's reaction.

"That's enough, Léonce! You can't really believe Lucette would steal anything in the house. How can you speak like that of your sister. You can be a real bastard at times."

Stunned by her words, Léonce stared at his wife. Never before had she dared to speak to him in that way. His face crimson with fury, he nearly raised his hand to her but regained control of himself in time realising everyone in the restaurant was watching them. He calmed down slowly and replied so that everyone could hear.

"You misunderstood me, my dear. I didn't intend to speak ill of my sister."

The waitress approached hesitantly with their first course. The couple smiled at her and made room on the table for her to serve them. They began to eat and the room breathed a sigh of relief or of disappointment depending on the table. Paul waited patiently for the second act to begin. He knew the drama was not finished yet.

After a few minutes Léonce began speaking again in a low voice.

"You know our mother inherited a collection of jewellery from her own mother. Elise kept them in her house for us. I simply want to get them back for you, Agnès. That's all."

"But the jewels must be shared with Lucette, I absolutely can't take them all myself," she whispered back.

"Of course, of course. That's what I meant."

The meal continued in silence and Paul remained near the fire reflecting on what he just heard.

Chapter 5

Monday, 19th September 1927

The next morning Léonce Beynard awoke around six o'clock in a bad mood. He had slept badly. Agnès was still sleeping soundly at his side, which irritated him all the more.

He looked out of the window. The rain of the previous evening had stopped and he decided to go for a walk around the village to clear his head before breakfast. He left the hotel and crossed the Place de la mairie, briefly acknowledging the grocer Leglu who was busy setting out his displays in front of the shop. He walked past the church before taking the path which led round the former grand house of the influential Béchade family and a group of other more modest houses before reaching the road to Coirac. He stopped for a moment deciding which direction to take, then turned left and set off to climb the hill up to the windmill called Cazault, which had only recently closed down. When he reached the mill he sat down on one of the large upturned millstones which had been abandoned outside and looked out over the vast flat valley stretching away below him.

All this countryside was not to his taste. He had become a real townsman, a solid bourgeois of Bordeaux, notary by profession, more at home in his office than out there in the fresh air at the mercy of the weather and the seasons. As if to confirm him in his opinion the wind got up and a sudden squall threw splatters of rain in his face. He wiped them off and headed back down the hill. He was in a hurry to return to the warmth of the hotel.

He intended to return to Bordeaux as soon as possible, but first they had to thoroughly search Elise's house to find the jewels, which he knew to be valuable. Having to share them with his younger sister was beyond annoying, but as Agnès had reminded him, as a notary, he knew he had no choice in the matter.

*

At ten o'clock Marie returned to Élise Coustaut's house as agreed with Lucette Marceau the evening before. She went in with a heavy heart. There was no-one there and it felt cold. She shivered. She was immediately aware of the emptiness and abandoned feel of the house. She hesitated. Should she light the fire in the hearth as she usually did? Would that be presumptuous? She was standing in the middle of the room trying to decide when Lucette entered.

"Bonjour, Marie. Thank you for coming, my dear," she said, kissing her on both cheeks. "It's cold in here. Would you light a fire, please?"

"With pleasure, madame, I was just wondering whether I should … "

"But of course! Francis will join us in an hour. He has to go somewhere first."

Lucette too could sense that indefinable atmosphere of a house no longer lived in. There was a special quality of silence, or rather absence of sound, as if the house itself was mourning and dying slowly. She shook off such thoughts and made herself form a plan of action. The heat from the fire was growing and beginning to invest the room. The house breathed again contentedly and emitted the usual sounds from the warming wooden beams. Life was returning.

"What would you like me to do, Madame Marceau?" Marie asked.

"To tell you the truth I don't know where to start, Marie! It's sad to have to sort out the personal effects of someone who has died so recently."

"You could wait, madame. Do it in a few days time when it's less painful perhaps."

"No, I can't. My brother will insist we start straight away. He won't wait, that's for sure. He'll be in a hurry to return to Bordeaux."

Right on cue Léonce entered the room with Agnès. He looked around as if to be sure he had entered the right house and then greeted his sister. He muttered a brief bonjour to Marie and immediately went over to the enormous walnut sideboard. Without a word he opened the drawers one after the other, rummaged inside and dumped the contents onto the floor when he couldn't find what he was looking for.

"Stop, Léonce! What on earth are you doing? We're not going to find the jewels that way," exclaimed Agnès.

"So what do you suggest?" he retorted.

"What jewels?" asked Lucette, amazed at her brother's behaviour.

"The jewels which belonged to our mother, of course and which Élise kept safe here. Valuable jewels acquired by our ancestors, who were members of the minor aristocracy under Napoleon III."

"What on earth are you talking about?" asked Lucette. "I've never heard anything about jewels or titles in the family. So I'm a baroness, am I?"

Léonce was suddenly aware Marie was standing there, not knowing what to do.

"Go and clean up the kitchen. This is none of your business," he snapped.

"Please," murmured Agnès.

"Of course ... please," Léonce mimicked.

Marie left the room and went into the kitchen hiding her anger and holding back her tears.

"Léonce! It's unacceptable to speak to her like that. She did so much to help Élise who took advantage of her for years. Our sister behaved abominably towards the girl, particularly after Gustave died."

"So. She could have resigned."

"You just don't understand, do you?" she replied exasperatedly.

"OK, that's enough. We're wasting time. We absolutely must find the jewels. You two have a look upstairs, I'm going to look in the attic."

The two women searched the rooms on the first floor. They opened cupboards, wardrobes and a whole collection of boxes and objects wrapped in tissue paper. They searched the pockets of coats and dresses, even shook out shoes.

Meanwhile Léonce abandoned the ground floor and went up into the attic. There were suitcases and trunks, and all manner of cardboard boxes. He tipped out the contents of every one more and more desperately. Finally he gave up and went down stairs to join the others.

All three were exhausted and could not understand where Élise could have hidden the jewels. They were certain she would not have deposited them in the bank for safe-keeping – *'better under the mattress',* she would have said. So they had to be somewhere in the house ... if they really do exist, Lucette said to herself.

"When was the last time you saw them, Léonce?" she asked.

"Frankly, I'm not sure. I was young, perhaps ten years old. Maman showed them to us, as if they were toys. Élise saw them, but you were too young to remember perhaps. Maman told us they came from our grandmother. She died – our grandmother I mean – in 1895, as you know."

He poured himself a coffee and pushed the cafetière towards his sisters.

"In reality," he continued, "it was our great-grandfather who made his fortune during the Second Empire as a member of the Assemblée Constituante of 1848. It must have been he who bought the jewels."

The two women looked at each other in amazement.

"I knew nothing about this. How did you find out?" asked Lucette.

"I already had a vague idea that great-grandfather, who was also called Léonce, was someone important, so I went to the library in Bordeaux and did some research."

"Do you know any more about him?"

"Well, a little. He was amongst those who voted to elect Louis-Napoleon Bonaparte president of the Second Republic. But after the coup d'etat in 1851 when Louis-Napoleon became Napoleon III and created the Second Empire I lost track of him."

"So, he didn't receive a title like many of the other supporters?" asked his wife.

"No, unfortunately not, my dear. You are not a baroness and I'm not a baron," he replied, smiling for the first time since their arrival.

"So where did the jewels come from?" asked Lucette.

"I don't know. But they exist. Great-grandfather must have bought them around that time, as I said."

"Would Élise have sold them? Or maman perhaps?"

"Maman? No, I don't think so. And Élise would have asked my advice, I'm sure. Besides they belong to us all not just to her."

All three fell silent, lost in their own thoughts. Suddenly Léonce stood up and shouted:

"Marie! Come here!"

Marie came into the room, frightened by the tone of his voice.

"Monsieur? "

"Tell me. Have you ever seen my sister's jewellery? Did she show them to you perhaps?"

"Non, monsieur. Madame didn't take me into her confidence."

"That's the least you could say," added Lucette. "She treated you very harshly, Marie. It was not fair of her."

"You don't have to apologise for our sister, Lucette, for goodness sake!" shot back Léonce.

"You are sure you never saw them. Tell me the truth."

"Non, monsieur, I promise you I have never seen any jewellery."

"Not even when you cleaned her room? You didn't open any drawers to see if there was something you could sell?"

"Léonce, stop!" demanded his wife.

"You can't accuse Marie like that of being a thief, Léonce," said Lucette. "I know her like my own daughter. She's not dishonest, I tell you. She is not a thief."

"How do you know? Were you here all the time? You have no idea what she did when she was alone in the house," he roared back.

Lucette went to put her arm round Marie, who was on the edge of tears, to comfort her, but she shrugged off her embrace and said to Beynard:

"Maître Beynard, I worked for your sister for four years. I have never seen any jewellery or anything else of value. I have never been in Madame's room, nor in Monsieur's. She did not allow it. I have never taken, stolen as you insinuate, anything whatever from the house. If you wish to accuse me of theft, then speak to my father, maître."

She turned towards the two women.

"Thank you for believing me, Madame Marceau, Madame Beynard. I'll leave you now."

She picked up her coat and went towards the door. Léonce looked as if he was going to prevent her from leaving, but his wife grabbed his arm and pulled him back.

Furious, he shouted:

"That's right! Just leave. That's really too easy."

He turned angrily to the two women who were silently applauding Marie.

"Peuh! It doesn't matter. She won't go far. We can find her easily enough. If we don't find the jewels, then she must have stolen them. Who else had a better opportunity to slip them out of the house? We must search her room immediately before she hides them somewhere else. If it's not too late already."

"Léonce, calm down. You have no proof. You are a solicitor. You know you can't lawfully search someone's house without a magistrate's permission," objected his wife. "Anyway, I simply don't believe it."

"Nor do I. First we must finish searching here in the house. There is still the barn and the garden. But I'll never believe Marie is a thief," said Lucette.

"OK, OK. You're right. But if we don't find them by the end of the day, I'll go to the police to ask for an official warrant to search her house. If she has nothing to fear, there will be no harm done."

"That's what you think. There will be rumours. She will have to leave the village as she will never get another job here. People are like that. It will be a disaster for her," said Lucette.

"So all you have to do is to find the jewels! So get to work!" he replied.

By the end of the day they were all convinced the jewels were not in the house. Léonce had even dug up the vegetable patch but to no avail.

"You're certain your mother didn't sell them some time ago, Léonce? It's possible, isn't it?" asked Agnès.

"No, I'm sure she couldn't have. It's not possible. Maman wouldn't have known how to. She would have asked me what to do."

"In that case," said Lucette, "we have to believe she was canny enough not to declare them to the tax people. There was no mention of them in her will after she died, was there?"

"So, we must ask the solicitor. He might know something," suggested Agnès.

"If she hid them, it's possible she didn't tell Élise where. She was very ill at the end," added Lucette.

"I hadn't thought of that. But I don't think so, Lucette. You're right, Agnès, we must check with maman's solicitor just in case."

"And ask at the bank. In Sauveterre or even Langon," said Agnès. "But if Lucette is right and Élise didn't know where the jewels were hidden, she couldn't have sold them either!"

"No, she did know, I'm certain. That bitch Marie stole them."

"Now you really have gone too far, Léonce. I can't allow you to use that foul word about Marie. If she hadn't looked after Élise all these years, it would have been you who would have had to pay dearly for her care in a home in Bordeaux," Agnès reminded him.

"OK, OK! You'll see I'm right in the end, but first I'll speak to the solicitor and the banks. I've had enough. Let's go back to the hotel. We'll start again tomorrow."

*

In the *Grand Hôtel* Paul was sitting in his usual place beside the fire in the bar. He was dozing after having spent a day of home visits to his patients. He was tired and deserved the few days off he was taking, starting the next day. He was planning to go to Bordeaux, back to his studio apartment in the Rue du Palais Gallien which he had kept since his days as a medical student at the university. He was counting on spending evenings out with friends from those days, on dining in good restaurants, on walking along the beach at Lacanau and on eating oysters in Arcachon,

He was also ticking off the days to the end of the week when he would drive to Biarritz to spend the weekend with his fiancée, Jacinthe, who was working there as a nurse and whom he had not seen for exactly nineteen days.

These pleasant plans running through his mind were brutally interrupted by the sound of the irritated voice of Léonce entering the bar with Agnès for dinner.

Paul didn't move a muscle, nor open his eyes, but he was wide awake and all ears. He heard the couple sit down at the same table as the evening before. They ordered without paying much attention again to their choices and seemed exhausted.

"Tomorrow we'll go to the solicitor and the banks, but if they have no information about the jewels as I suspect, I'll demand a warrant to search the house of that girl."

"Her name is Marie, Léonce. Alright, you do as you wish, but I don't agree with you and I'm worried about the effect on that poor young woman and on her father. You have no proof she has stolen anything and you will ruin her life."

The couple didn't speak again during the meal and finally left the table in silence. Paul was turning over in his mind what he had heard. He had an idea of what they were discussing from having visited the Coustaut house so many times. His predecessor had spoken to him about his suspicion that Élise, Léonce and Lucette had inherited something of great value in 1906 on the death of their mother and which had not been declared to the tax authorities. So, it seemed it was jewellery, judging by what he had overheard.

But what was this talk of searching Marie's home? He wondered. Surely they didn't suspect her of stealing the jewels? But that was the obvious conclusion to draw from their conversation.

He stood up abruptly and went out to his motorcar.

He knocked on the door and waited. A voice from inside demanded to know who was there at this late hour. He gave his name. Lucette opened the door immediately and invited him in. After half an hour Paul Lasserre left the house and went to see the mayor.

Chapter 6

Tuesday, 20th September 1927

The following day the mayor approached the Grand Hôtel. He went into the dining room, but there was no-one there. He ordered a coffee and waited. After a quarter of an hour Agnès Beynard came in and sat at her table. The waiter served her a bowl of coffee and put a basket of bread and croissants on the table.

The mayor approached and greeted her.

"Bonjour, Madame Beynard. May I speak with you for a moment?"

"Bonjour, Monsieur le maire. Of course. Please join me."

"Merci, madame."

He sat down and looked round.

"Don't worry. My husband has already left to go to see the solicitor and the bank in Langon. What would you like to speak to me about?"

"It's delicate, madame, but ... "

" ... you have heard that my husband suspects Marie Bourdet of having stolen some jewels from my sister-in-law. Is that it?"

"Yes, that's exactly what I heard. I appreciate your directness. Without wishing to be indiscreet, I have the impression you don't share your husband's suspicions. Am I mistaken?"

"Not at all. We have searched everywhere in poor Élise's house, but we haven't found any jewels. To suspect such a devoted young woman of having stolen them simply because we can't find them is absurd."

"I understand there is no proof Marie has taken them?"

"None at all. I asked my husband to go and see the solicitor to find out if he knows anything. Élise may have sold them, always supposing she knew where they were after their mother died seventeen years ago. And I asked him to ask at the bank if she had deposited them there."

"And if he does not find out anything, will he still want a search of the Bourdet house?"

"I'm sure he will. Can you do anything to prevent it, Monsieur le maire? It will be a catastrophe for Marie and for her poor widowed father."

"You mean there will still be rumours even if the search almost certainly yields nothing?"

"You see how easily it starts! You said 'almost certainly', Monsieur le maire."

"True. I'm sorry. It was just a turn of phrase, but you are right, that's how rumours start."

He fell silent and Agnès waited while he gathered his thoughts. He ordered another coffee for them both. Finally he decided on a plan.

"Here's what I propose, Madame Beynard. As mayor, one of my duties is being responsible for the police, as you know. Let's suppose your husband is not successful at the notaire's nor at the bank, are you sure he will still insist on accusing Marie? Even without definite proof?"

"Yes, absolutely, Monsieur le maire."

"In that case without reasonable grounds I can't grant an official search warrant. I'll suggest he goes to talk to Antoine Bourdet as discreetly as possible, but only in my presence. Better I go with him than that he goes alone."

"Merci, Monsieur le maire. I appreciate what you propose. But I admit I'm still worried for Marie and her father. Let's hope the jewels are in the bank or with the solicitor and that the matter will be resolved without the need for a visit."

"I sincerely hope so too, Madame Beynard."

Chapter 7

Wednesday, 21st September 1927

"Have you heard what happened at Antoine's this morning, Aristide?" asked his wife when the young mason returned that evening.

He looked at her in surprise and sank down into his favourite chair.

"No, Georgette. I don't have time to stop every three minutes to listen to the latest gossip from the village. I was working."

"Calm down!" she replied, as she continued to prepare the evening meal. "Just wait. You'll be interested. The mayor went with Léonce Beynard to search Antoine's house."

"What? What are you nattering about, woman?"

"It's true. Beynard suspects Marie of having stolen poor Élise's jewels."

"What rubbish! Marie is a good girl. She put up for too long with the evil little ways of that bitter woman."

Georgette stirred the stew in the casserole before replying.

"Bitter, maybe, Aristide, but life has treated her badly all the same. Gustave was never the same after he returned wounded from the war."

"Nobody is the same after that bloody war," he said banging his fist on the table. "He's not the only one to have suffered."

He fell silent for a moment.

"So exactly what happened at Antoine's? Should I go and see him?"

"Are so now you do want to know! I didn't think you listened to gossip!"

Smiling, he mimed the slap which he threatened to give her.

"Listen, Aristide. It's serious. Beynard accused her of having taken the jewels because he can't find them in his sister's house. It seems he looked everywhere with Lucette and Agnès. He thinks the only explanation is that Marie stole them. So he demanded a search of Marie's room and of the whole house."

"But that's scandalous! The fact he can't find them isn't proof Marie stole them, for heaven's sake."

"Exactly, but Léonce insisted on the search and the mayor did what he could to limit the damage, but it's a catastrophe for Marie and Antoine."

"No-one likes the brother in the village. People aren't going to believe his accusations, surely?"

"Perhaps not, but the humiliation will be too much for Antoine and there are always those who believe there's no smoke without fire, as the saying goes. Marie will never find work in the village after having been accused of theft. And poor Antoine, all this on top of having closed down the mill."

"What? He's no longer working?"

"No, he stopped when the grape harvest was all in. Haven't you noticed his windmill is no longer turning? Nor Philippe's? You really do have your head buried in your boots."

"I was busy at the château. But you're right, I should have noticed. It's sad," he added getting up and taking his place at the table. "The windmills of Gonin are the reason the village exists, they're history, tradition."

"True. But everything's changing now. They say it's progress," she replied, serving him a plate of stew and sitting at the table opposite him.

"Heu! What progress?" he said, beginning to eat. "Is that what we fought for during the war?"

*

Scandalised by his attitude and his accusation against Marie and her father, Lucette and Agnès refused to accompany Léonce to Antoine Bourdet's.

The miller refused at first to let Beynard enter, but the mayor persuaded him it was better to accept the search than to refuse. Since there was nothing to find, that would be the end of the matter.

After Beynard had left empty-handed and furious, the mayor stayed to speak to Antoine and Marie.

"Marcel, tell me why you allowed that brute to humiliate us like that?" asked Antoine. "You and I have been friends for years. How could you have allowed this? You can't really believe your god-daughter is a thief. I'm just grateful my poor Louise is not here to see this."

Marie put her arms round her father to comfort him. Both of them had tears of fury and humiliation running down their cheeks.

"Of course not, Antoine. But Beynard threatened to ask for an official search warrant," he replied. "He's a solicitor and has contacts in high places. He could have had you both arrested and placed in custody while an investigation was started. I did what I could to protect you. Since he has no proof of course, I persuaded him to make an unofficial visit and to let me come with him as witness."

"Do you think it's really over? He's not going to come back?" asked Marie.

"I don't know frankly, Marie. He's a difficult and obstinate man. All I can do now to go and speak to Agnès and Lucette again. They are the only ones who can persuade him to drop the accusation."

*

On Thursday, market day, Marie went into Gornac to do her shopping as usual. Everyone in the village knew about the events of the day before. Everyone was aware the search of their house had revealed nothing and everyone said that of course they believed she was innocent. But a lingering doubt had taken root in people's minds.

Marie was overwhelmed with sadness that even those who had known her since she was a little girl were now unsure.

She wandered amongst the stalls to choose her vegetables, fruit, bread and a little meat as she had done every week since the death of her mother. Louise Bourdet had taught her daughter well how to choose carefully and how to spend her money to the best effect. She approached the stall where her mother had always bought their vegetables and to which Marie had remained faithful. She greeted the stall-holder cheerfully.

"Bonjour, Monsieur Moustié. How are you? And how is your wife? Has she recovered from her cold?"

He grunted a vague reply and avoided catching her eye. After a moment of embarrassment, realising he didn't want to talk to her, she asked:

"A kilo of potatoes, please."

He weighed the potatoes on the scales and emptied them into the basket she held out for him. Marie handed him the money, which he took, again without looking at her. She moved away quickly to avoid him seeing she was in tears and was almost knocked over by a young lad who was running around the market weaving in and out of the people around her, causing her to drop her basket. Some of the potatoes spilt out and she bent down to pick them up. No-one stopped to help her.

She sensed everyone was watching to see if she was spending more than she usually did in the market, whether her basket was fuller than normal. Was she buying herself a little luxury today?

She knew that as soon as she was out of hearing tongues were wagging behind her back. 'How can she afford all that? Her poor father is no longer working, so where's the money coming from?' they asked each other.

She tried to act as if nothing had changed and greeted people as she always did every day. She did not receive many responses in return and often people avoided catching her eye.

At a meat stall the butcher went on talking to the customer in front of her for so long she understood he didn't want to serve her. She walked away to find another stall-holder who was prepared to sell her what she was looking for.

Finally she could stand it no more. She left the market , tears in her eyes.

Chapter 8

Saturday, 15th October 1927

It was late in the evening. Marie was sitting alone on the mound leaning up against the base of the windmill. She was starting to feel cold and was thinking of going back to the house when she heard a sound behind her. Alain appeared from behind the windmill.

"Alain! It's so good to see you. Thank you, thank you for coming. How did you know I was here?"

He kissed her gently on the lips and sat down close beside her. He had brought a blanket and put it round both their shoulders to protect them from the cold. For a while they remained side by side not saying a word, feeling the warmth from each others' bodies.

"I heard what happened at the market on Thursday," he said.

"It's all becoming too much," she said, unable to stop herself letting it all out. "Without you, I couldn't go on. Papa is completely shattered. He's becoming more and more depressed and weak. He hardly eats and doesn't dare go out into the village any more. He's afraid of what people will say. He thinks they're talking behind his back. And he's right.

"He went into the village a few days ago and wanted to play cards as usual with his friends in the café, but all the tables were full and no-one said hello. He came back home alone and so sad. Alain, it's over for us in the village, all because of that bastard Beynard!"

Alain pulled her closer and kissed her on the cheek.

"I know the mayor and Dr Lasserre are doing everything they can to help us and to tell everyone the accusation is false, that Beynard is wrong and the jewels are lost or were even sold. But people are still talking. I can't take it any more, Alain."

"I know it's horrible for you, but it'll pass. People will forget. There'll be another drama, another person they can gossip about. You'll see."

"Perhaps, but in the meantime it's breaking my heart to see papa like this. I'm afraid for him. Dr Lasserre says he can do nothing more for him and that I must persuade him to go out and meet people. But his friends have deserted him, so what can I do?"

"Have you thought of asking Lucette Marceau? She could help by coming to see your father. They have been friends since they were children. You know, my father told me she was the prettiest girl in the village when he was young and all the boys wanted to step out with her, including your father. They gave up hope when she made it clear she would marry Albert Marceau."

"Yes, I know. I think papa is still a bit in love with her. At least *she* believes me and she has been several times to the house, but nothing works. I think if it continues like this he'll die of shame and loneliness. It's not my fault. I haven't done anything wrong. I didn't steal those bloody jewels!"

He hugged her, stroking her cheek and her hair and turned her face to look at him.

"You do know I believe you, don't you, my sweet? We must be patient. It will pass. Trust me."

"Perhaps, but apart from you I feel so alone and I'm afraid. I want to leave the village, go to Bordeaux, find a job but I can't leave papa."

"And what about me?"

"Nor you."

It was dark and cold but they did not move. The stars picking out the constellations were shining brightly and the Milky Way was spreading its soft shawl around them. But Alain and Marie paid no attention to the display above them. A sky full of inexplicable marvels is no surprise to those who live in the countryside where a clear night sky brimming with sparkling stars is the norm.

They wondered rather what the future held for them, knowing the answer was not in the stars but on the earth below.

Chapter 9

Sunday, 11th December 1927

The funeral of the former miller was held two weeks before Christmas. He had hardly eaten for weeks before and had become weaker and weaker despite the desperate efforts of his daughter. Lucette had come to help Marie every day towards the end, but Antoine had lost the will to live. He died on St Nicholas Day aged only 45. The last word he uttered was that of his wife Louise.

He had been well respected in the village and on the day of his funeral the accusation against him and Marie seemed to have been forgotten or at least set aside. Mourners came to the funeral from several villages around and the day passed in an atmosphere of sadness, respect and dignity. Later in front of the church Marie received the condolences expected.

Afterwards at the wake at the house the normal customs were observed and no mention was made of the jewels. But nonetheless they were on everyone's mind. Marie had the impression all eyes were roaming around the room observing the furniture and looking for likely places where the jewels could be hidden.

Paul Lasserre had been present at the funeral service of his friend and was impressed by the number of people who had come to pay their respects. He spent his time during the service watching those who had come to honour Bourdet's memory. Paul was sure that in the past the majority had bought their flour direct from the door of Antoine's mill, but that had not prevented them from suspecting him of having profited from the sale of the jewels belonging to the widow Coustaut and of using his daughter to steal them.

Despite there being no proof, the rumours had been enough to condemn them both. Nevertheless, either because of the demands of their faith or from simple curiosity here they were at the funeral service. He had no doubt they would go to the wake afterwards.

'What a catastrophe for Marie', he thought. 'She has lost her father and in consequence the house where she was born. What will become of her?'

Coming out of the church and waiting in the queue to offer his condolences to Marie, he made up his mind to talk to Bernard Duvigneau, Alain's father. 'He's a fair man who has always liked Marie. He'll certainly have some ideas about how we can help her.'

When his turn came he kissed Marie on both cheeks and whispered to her not to worry. He wouldn't abandon her and would find a way to help her.

After everyone had left Lucette and Francis stayed to help Marie clear up. When it was done and everything put away Lucette sat beside Marie and took her hand.

"I'm sorry, but you know you can't stay in the house now, Marie. It's part of the tenancy agreement your father had with the owner of the windmill. The house now reverts back to the owner."

"I know. Monsieur Grive has given me a week's grace to find somewhere else. Then I must leave the house, but I don't know what to do. What will happen to me, Madame Marceau? I have no money and papa had nothing to leave me. I'd like to go to Bordeaux to find a job as a maid, but this accusation will follow me there. No-one will hire me, I know. And I'd kill myself rather than sell my body like a prostitute!"

"Calm yourself, Marie. There is no question of that. I have already discussed this with Paul. You will come to live with

Francis and me while he finds you a job in Bordeaux. He knows lots of people in the city and he will definitely find you something suitable."

Marie burst into tears and put her arms round Lucette who hugged her tightly and stroked her hair, calming her down.

"How can I thank you enough, Madame Marceau?" she said through her tears. "You and the doctor are the only ones who believe me."

"Not at all, Marie. I know Alain and his parents believe you. You have more friends in the village than you think. We are going to help you, I promise you."

She gently released herself from Marie's arms and stood up. She looked down with great kindness at this young woman who was so struck down with grief and worry.

"Francis and I are going to leave you now. Put your things together and everything you wish to keep. Tomorrow morning Francis will come and fetch you and you will come to stay with us. We'll discuss more tomorrow, but you can live with us as long as you wish, my dear."

She kissed her good-bye and she and Francis left the house. Marie remained sitting, enveloped in the silence of her home, surrounded by fears and memories.

*

The same evening Paul entered the Duvigneau house and followed the winemaker into the main room. The Duvigneau family had been winemakers for several generations in the village. Having three sons and three daughters, this head of the family had done his duty as he saw it to ensure the continuation of the family. The name Duvigneau would not die out any time soon.

Short in stature and stocky, used as he was to manual work, Bernard Duvigneau nonetheless had a distinguished air about him. He liked to think his family had its origins in the nobility, but had never been able to find any evidence. What he did know was that an ancestor had accompanied the Marquis de LaFayette in 1780 on the frigate Hermione to go and help the Americans to rid themselves of the English oppressor and win their independence.

Towards the end of the nineteenth century another branch of the family had emigrated to Québec where they settled in Chicoutimi, a town whose origins lay in being a trading post for French trappers and local Indians who hunted beaver for their skins. He was proud of his adventurous cousins and had always remained in contact by letter.

"Bienvenue, Paul! What can I do for you?" he asked, after handing him a glass of white wine.

"Merci, Bernard," he said, accepting the glass.

He showed his appreciation of the dry white wine from Bernard's vineyard with a nod after taking a sip.

"I've come to talk to you about Marie Bourdet, as you have no doubt guessed."

"Yes. The poor girl. What will she do now? I presume she has to leave the house now her father had died."

"Yes. Antoine was just a tenant. But as far as that is concerned there's no problem. She's going to live with Lucette Marceau and her son."

"Excellent! So Madame Marceau doesn't believe this infamous story of the theft of the jewels either?"

"Not at all. You know Léonce Beynard is her brother? It's no doubt to make up for his disappointment at not having found the jewels, which he hoped to inherit and receive a goodly sum for, that he has turned his fury onto Marie and her father without any regard for the damage he's doing."

"And the result is she has no chance now of finding a job in the village?"

"Exactly."

"She's a young woman I have great affection for. She's been here to help with the harvest a couple of times, you know. And," he added with a smile, "I know Alain wants to marry her!"

"He's told you?"

"Not yet, but he does. I know, I'm his father!"

"And what do you think about that?"

"Oh, I'd be delighted. The Bourdets are a old and honourable family of millers. I have no objection."

"And what about Simone? She would be pleased too?"

"Of course. She likes Marie and wants more grand-children!"

"You've two other sons. Haven't they produced enough grand-children for her already?"

Bernard laughed.

"You'd think so. But no. We have seven grand-children already and it goes on. Our daughters are going to contribute to the total soon!"

"Congratulations. But what about Alain … ?"

"You mean, what are his future prospects? He has two older brothers. The vineyard cannot support three growing families. Is that what you're wondering?"

"Yes, if you have no objection to my question."

"Not at all."

The two men looked at each other without saying any more. Each knew what the other was thinking. Paul broached the subject first.

"So. When they are ready, you give them permission to marry, but in the circumstances they can't stay here. You offer Alain the value of his share of the vineyard or at least you offer to support them financially for a certain time, but not here."

"Say I do what you suggest, where will they go?"

He said nothing for a moment looking at Paul who was waiting for him to arrive at the answer for himself without being prompted.

"You've already thought of a solution, haven't you? So, tell me! Not just to Bordeaux, surely?"

Bernard searched his face trying to read the answer in his expression.

"Of course!" he said suddenly, banging his forehead with his fist. "Go to the cousins in Québec and start over? That's what you're thinking?"

"Yes."

"That would be hard for us. Losing a son like him, the youngest and his mother's favourite, wouldn't be easy," he replied slowly. "But it would be a great opportunity for them," he added, agreeing with Paul the more he thought it through.

"You'll have to discuss it with Simone first, Bernard. It's a decision you must arrive at together."

"Of course, but she will agree. Like me she's in contact with our cousins. They are good people and I'm sure they will take care of Alain and Marie. And it wouldn't be for ever, they'll be able to return if they wish later when all this silly business has died down and been forgotten."

Paul said nothing further but raised his glass to his host with a smile.

*

The next morning Francis Marceau arrived at the house in his motorcar. He was fond of Marie and was furious with his uncle for having made her situation in the village so impossible. He was disappointed with those in the village who believed a young woman they had known all her life could suddenly become a jewel thief. Especially when there was absolutely no proof she was guilty or even that the jewels existed.

He knew how difficult it was to be an orphan. For him, it was his father he had lost. For Marie, her mother. He was proud of his mother for having invited Marie to come to live with them as long as she wanted, but he knew it was only a temporary solution. Marie probably had no choice but to leave the village if she was to find work. Luckily there were still enough people in the village who were willing to help her. He just hoped they would find some way for her to be able to stay after all.

He jumped down from the motorcar and knocked on the door. Marie opened it and invited him in. Francis kissed her on both cheeks and went inside. He could see she had been crying. In the centre of the main room she had piled up her belongings in boxes and a suitcase.

"Is that all?" he asked, surprised at how little she wanted to take with her.

"Yes. I'll come back tomorrow to sort out papa's clothes. Honestly, I just can't do it today. I'll perhaps be able to sell some of his things at the market on Thursday. He didn't have much. As for the furniture, I'm going to leave that for the next tenant. Unless you or your mother would like anything. You are going to be married soon, so if you need anything ..."

"We'll talk about it later at the house, Marie. Right, let's load your things into the motorcar. Maman is waiting. You are going to be the daughter she never had and for me the sister I never had. We'll be able to celebrate Christmas together as a family."

With tears in her eyes Marie hugged him like the brother she had always wanted. After helping him to load the motorcar, she took a last look round and locked the door.

Chapter 10

Saturday, 31st December 1927

Bernard Duvigneau had invited her to come for an apéritif just before La fête du Saint Sylvestre. Lucette was not fooled in the least. She had guessed it was to talk about Marie. She was not surprised either to find Paul Lasserre there too. Simone Duvigneau greeted her at the door and took her into the main room where the two men were waiting accompanied by Alain. Simone served them all a vin d'épices from the vineyard and took her seat next to Lucette.

The discussion lasted an hour.

"Madame Marceau," said Alain, his voice betraying his nervousness. "I still haven't talked to Marie about this plan as you know of course. I wanted to be sure in my own mind first that it was the right choice. Going so far away and leaving the family is an enormous decision.

"But after talking it over with my parents and my brothers, I realised it would be a fantastic adventure for the two of us and it wouldn't necessarily be for ever. We would always have the opportunity to return to France if it didn't work out. I know too that our cousins will help us. We have discussed the possibility with them and they are already preparing a fabulous welcome for us."

He paused to steady his voice.

"I know you are very fond of Marie, madame, and so I want you to be happy too in your own mind that it's the right decision before I ask Marie if she will marry me and if she will agree to starting a new life in Québec."

He stopped and breathed a sigh of relief that he had said all he wanted to without hesitating, despite the words having all tumbled out so quickly. He wasn't used to talking for so long in front of so many people. But by stating the plan out loud he realised he had definitely made up his mind and come to a decision.

Lucette smiled. She too realised that he had made his decision.

"Thank you, Alain. I appreciate all you have said. I'm very fond of Marie, and like you and your family, I don't believe this ridiculous accusation my brother has made against her. The plan you have in mind and the financial support you are offering them, Monsieur Duvigneau, is very generous.

"I'm sure Marie wants to marry you, Alain, you needn't worry on that score, and I am equally certain she will be over the moon at the idea of going to Québec and starting a new life ..."

She hesitated for a moment and took a sip of the wine which she had hardly touched during the discussion.

"But ..." completed Simone gently.

"But we mustn't spring this on her too soon. Her father died only a month ago. She is slowly accepting it, but she is still fragile."

"What do you propose, Lucette?" asked Paul.

"I suggest Alain wait a few days more and that he come to the house for the Fête des Rois."

"What an excellent idea, madame," exclaimed Bernard. "I know how much you love and protect this courageous young woman. My wife and I too feel great affection for her. She has come to work in the vineyard at harvest time more than once, as you know, and we know her to be spirited and honest. We will be delighted to welcome her into the family."

He stood up, signalling the end of the discussion.

" So. A toast! To the Fête des Rois!"

1928

Chapter 11

Friday, 6th January 1928

At midday on the day of the Fête des Rois, Alain knocked gingerly on the door of the house. Lucette opened it and invited him in.

She greeted him and whispered:

"She doesn't know you're coming today, Alain. But I'm sure she'll guess why you're here as soon as she sees you! Good luck, but I'm certain she will say yes."

In the small dining-room Lucette had laid the table for the festive meal. Francis and his young wife Eugénie were already sitting at the table and stood up to greet Alain, just as Marie came into the room and smiled with delight when she saw him.

"Bonjour, Alain," she said, blushing when he kissed her. "I didn't know you were coming. That's kind of you Madame Lucette to have invited Alain."

"He's very welcome," she replied, indicating to them to take their places. "It's all ready. Help yourselves to soup. Oh! I've forgotten the bread."

"I'll go," said Marie, getting up.

"No, I'll go. You two are the honoured guests today," said Francis.

Lucette gave him a furious look to stop him saying any more and, grinning, he went to fetch the bread.

During the meal they talked about everything and nothing in particular: the village gossip, the quality of the white wine of the previous year which was now bottled and thought promising. Lucette and Eugénie chatted about family matters and Marie was content to sit quietly listening to Francis and Alain discussing the new cars in the village: the Renault B2 half van of the pharmacist and particularly the yellow Citroen C3 of Monsieur Mares, nicknamed the Cloverleaf because there was only one seat in the back. At Château Espère Monsieur Coiffard also had a motorcar, as did Paul Lasserre and Francis himself.

"I'd like to buy a motorcar one day," said Alain. "Papa has bought a Citroen van B15 for the vineyard – practical but not very stylish! At least now I can learn to drive."

"You can learn on mine too if you like."

"That's good of you, Francis. Thank you."

After the main course Lucette and Marie cleared the table while the others continued to chat and carried the plates into the kitchen. Marie was still curious to know why she had invited Alain to the meal, but Lucette pretended not to have heard the question and handed Marie the Gâteau des Rois to take to the table.

"Who will be the king or queen today, I wonder," asked Lucette, cutting slices of the cake and putting them on the plates.

When everyone was served, Francis opened a bottle of champagne and filled their glasses. He raised a toast:

"To the future. May it bring happiness and riches to us all."

Alain bit into his piece of cake and his teeth closed on the 'bean'.

"Excellent! I'm the King!" he said. "Everyone must do as I command."

He hesitated and then took the plunge.

"I command you three to leave me alone with Marie for five minutes."

"Alain! But you can't do that! It's not polite," objected Marie, still unaware of his intentions.

"But I'm King for the day! It's the tradition."

"Of course. At your command, Majesty," said Lucette standing up and indicating to Francis and Eugénie to follow her. "But five minutes only. That's all," she added with a smile.

The three of them left the dining room to Marie's amazement and went into the kitchen.

Francis took advantage of the pause to prepare the coffee and Lucette went to fetch a second bottle of champagne from the cellar. Eugénie was starting the washing up when they heard a squeal from the dining room.

"It's done," said Lucette. "We can go back in. Bring the champagne, Francis."

Chapter 12

Saturday, 14th April 1928

Their wedding took place on April 14th, a week after Easter. The rain that day was exceptionally heavy and the couple had to run across the market square from the motorcar into the mairie. Only the families were present. Nonetheless it was a happy and noisy ceremony. Alain's two brothers and two sisters arrived with their children, eight in total, including the latest by one of his sisters. Lucette, Francis and Eugénie, and Paul Lasserre contributed to the atmosphere and the noise. But when the young couple came out of the mairie after the signing of the registers only a few close friends of the Duvigneau family were waiting outside in the square to greet them.

Marie wondered how it could be that the villagers were so convinced of her guilt they did not come to wish them well as was the custom. But she was so happy on the arm of her young husband that she preferred not to dwell on such thoughts. So it was only the delighted family and friends who wished to support them who accompanied the couple across the square to the church.

The church ceremony lasted an hour and afterwards the guests walked to the Duvigneau's house for the reception. It was a happy occasion, but tinged with a certain mood of sadness. Alain's mother could not help herself bursting into tears, knowing she would no longer see her son for possibly several years.

"Don't cry, maman, You can come and see us, it's not difficult now. The liners are amazing and very quick – they take only six or seven days to cross the Atlantic. The cousins will be delighted to see you. And we will come back. We're not going for ever!"

"But it's so far, my dear. I'm going to miss you."

"I'll miss the whole family, maman. But it'll be a fantastic opportunity for us. Uncle André has already offered me a job and we're going to buy a motorcar there – definitely more stylish than the one papa has! – as soon as we have saved enough money."

"And they've found us a house to rent," said Marie. "We'll have lots of room for you, madame, and for Monsieur Duvigneau too of course!"

"And there are vineyards in Québec, so we won't feel too far from home. Maybe I'll be able to buy one one day. Think of that, a Duvigneau vineyard in Québec!"

"But it's so cold there. Minus 50 degrees in winter I've heard. How is that possible? How can people exist in that?" asked Lucette. "Are you sure you have enough coats and gloves?"

"Don't worry, Madame Marceau," replied Alain. "Our cousins will take good care of us. It will still be summer when we arrive and we'll have plenty of time to prepare for the winter."

"But there are wolves and bears and wild Indians … ", said his mother.

"That's enough, maman! It's not a barbarian country. It's French, so nothing to worry about."

Bernard came up to them smiling.

"I see the ladies are worried and trying to frighten you, children. Too late! The decision had been taken This will be a amazing adventure for you both. I'm even a little jealous myself!"

"I've heard that it will be possible soon for anyone to telephone from Québec to France," said Alain.

"That's good news," said Francis, who was looking at his watch, "but we must be leaving soon if I'm to take you to the station in Saint Brice in time."

"Right. You're going to spend two nights in a hotel in Bordeaux," said Bernard, looking at the documents in his hand. "The room is booked. After that you'll take the train to Paris. Here are the tickets – one way! I have booked a hotel there for ten days. It will be your first visit to the capital, so you must take full advantage of the time you have there. Then you'll take the train for Cherbourg on the coast, where you'll wait for the liner Ausonia to arrive from Southampton in England. It leaves for Queenstown in America before going on to Québec."

Marie listened to all the details with astonishment, hardly able to believe what she was hearing. For a young woman who had never travelled further than Sauveterre de Guyenne all of 8 kilometres away on the new bus service from Gornac this journey seemed like a fairy tale.

"How can I thank you, Monsieur and Madame Duvigneau? It's like a dream," she said, throwing her arms round both of them.

She looked across to Paul Lasserre who was watching the scene, a glass in hand.

"All you have to do to thank us, my dear daughter-in-law, is to make our son happy. I'm confident you will do that," replied her father-in-law, putting his arm round her.

He turned to Alain.

"Here are all the documents, my son. Everything you will need for the journey. Give our best to our cousins and be sure to write to us as soon as you can."

*

On their arrival at Bordeaux-Passerelle station they took a taxi to their hotel with their luggage. Marie was amazed at all the activity going on around them. The city seemed enormous to her and she simply couldn't comprehend the number of people in the streets.

"What do all these people do? They can't all work here."

"But of course they do! It's here the wine agents sell the wine produced in Gornac and the other villages. Look over there! That's the Garonne. There are warehouses all along the embankment. Our wines are exported to countries all around the world. Even to Québec!"

"So we could buy your father's wine there? That would be amazing!"

"True," said Alain. "But here's the hotel."

They got out of the taxi and the driver helped them carry their luggage into the hotel foyer. Alain approached the reception desk. He had already spent several nights in Bordeaux with his father on past visits, but this was his first time as head of the family.

Marie blushed as she signed the register, hesitating for a second before writing 'Madame Marie Duvigneau' while glancing at her husband out of the corner of her eye. The receptionist pretended not to notice her embarrassment, but she couldn't resist a smile.

"You'd better get used to it, my sweet. It's your name now," Alain whispered.

In the bedroom, which she thought very luxurious, Marie sat on the edge of the bed and watched Alain opening a suitcase and pulling out some clothes.

"Alain, I'm afraid. What if we bump into that man Beynard in the street?"

"No chance! Bordeaux is a huge city. There are thousands of people here. There's no way we'll meet him by accident. You'll see. It's going to be great. We'll go to see the cathedral and the museum and eat in nice restaurants. We're going to walk along the embankment and perhaps even take a boat trip. Don't worry, my pretty one. Beynard can't do us any harm now. You're my wife and I'm here to protect you."

Marie leaned over to give him a kiss and then helped him unpack their clothes. Despite what Alain had said and however reassuring he was, she still felt nervous.

'Is it the possibility of meeting Léonce Beynard which is making me nervous or is it the thought of our wedding night which is bothering me?' she wondered as she hung her dresses in the wardrobe.

Glancing across at her young and handsome husband, she added: 'Well, it's definitely not the wedding night!'

Chapter 13

Sunday, 15th April 1928

Marie awoke late the next morning. She was alone in a large bed. Puzzled, she looked round the room she found herself in. There was a wardrobe, a table, two chairs and a door which led to the *'salle de bains attenante'* – something she had never seen or even imagined before and which seemed to her to be the ultimate in luxury.

The sun's rays filtered through the curtains illuminating the room in a yellow glow. The open window carried the noise of the traffic and the cries of the merchants in the street below up to her. With a smile she remembered where she was and remembered the love-making of the previous night, of their wedding night.

"So," she said aloud, now completely awake, "I'm no longer in Gornac! I've just spent the night in Bordeaux in a hotel for the first time in my life. I'm no longer Marie Bourdet, daughter of a miller, maid of all work. I'm Madame Marie Duvigneau on the way with my husband to Québec!"

She was about to get out of the bed when the door opened and Alain entered holding a tray with two bowls of coffee and a basket of croissants.

"Stay there, my sweet. This morning we're having breakfast in bed. We're in no hurry. The day is ours to do whatever we wish and the city is ours to explore."

He approached the bed and put the tray on the bedside table. Marie made room for him and he stretched out beside her. He reached out to put his arms round her, but she pushed him away laughing.

"No! That's enough! I'm hungry and I want to go out and explore the town. It's such a beautiful day and besides you had enough of me last night."

"Never enough, my sweet," he said, moving across again to kiss her.

"But the coffee will go cold, Alain and ... "

" ... you see? I told you the coffee would be disgusting. *Enfin, bon!* We're going into town now and you're going to buy me a proper coffee in a classy restaurant to make up for it."

She jumped out of bed, dodged his outstretched arms attempting to entrap her, grabbed one of the croissants as she went by and escaped into the bathroom locking the door behind her.

Alain remained lying back in the bed hands behind his head reflecting on what the future held for them. Leaving the village where he was born and emigrating to Québec was a huge decision, but he knew it was also a great opportunity. He had much to think about.

Life in the countryside was still difficult even ten years after the Grande Guerre. France was recovering slowly, but there was an atmosphere, particularly in the towns, of a wish to forget, of a desire to let go and to be wildly, beautifully, irresponsible. In Paris American music – jazz, they called it – was all the rage. Most of the population just wanted to lose themselves completely in dance, song and entertainment. It was all a reaction to the horrors of the war, he knew. But not foresighted.

Others, more thoughtful, were concerned about what was happening on the other side of the Rhine with the forming of a party of the extreme right, even if it called itself 'socialist' and the rise in the opinion polls of its leader.

These dark thoughts were interrupted by the young woman who came out of the bathroom, fully dressed and ready to go out into the town.

"You're so pretty!"

"Thank you young man. Do I know you?"

She pulled him out of the bed, gave him a quick kiss and pushed him into the bathroom.

"Hurry up! I want to go out. And remember you owe me a proper hot coffee."

*

"So, how was the wedding in the village of the two young people you told me about?" asked Jacinthe.

The two lovers were walking arm in arm in the Botanical Gardens in the pleasant April sun. Paul had told his fiancée he had been invited to the wedding in Gornac of two young people who wished to emigrate to Canada.

"It all went well," he replied.

"That's it? It's a wedding. I want every detail, please! What was the bride's dress like? And the groom? What did he wear? Who did he choose as his witness? Did all the family go? Were lots of the villagers there? Tell me everything! Men!"

She pinched him on the arm to encourage him.

"Well, Marie wore a dress … "

" … good!"

" … which was white."

"Well, that's unusual!"

"Alain wore a dark suit. All the family came to the *mairie* and to the church. Afterwards we went to the parents' house for the reception. That's it."

"Great! Now I know everything. You are have the gift of observation, Paul. *Enfin bon*, so tell me about the reception."

"Bernard Duvigneau, Alain's father, gave them two nights in a hotel in Bordeaux and several nights in Paris for their honeymoon. Then they will go to Cherbourg and wait for the arrival of the liner which will take them to Québec. He has booked a cabin for them for the voyage."

"That's fantastic! What a dream for the two of them, but above all for Marie. From being a simple village girl to being transformed overnight into a young bride and overseas traveller, that's amazing. Has she ever left Gornac before?"

"She has never been any further than Sauveterre de Guyenne before!"

"What a great adventure for her. Tell me again why they've decided to emigrate."

"Ah!"

Paul hesitated, not wanting to reveal the real reason. One day perhaps when the mystery is solved, he thought.

"It's partly because there still isn't much work or many opportunities in the countryside, even ten years after the war. Bernard has two other sons who work in the vineyard and he received an invitation from his cousins in Québec mentioning a job that could interest Alain. For the two young people it was an offer not to be missed."

"I agree, it's a great opportunity, but their parents are going to miss them. Québec is a long way away," said Jacinthe.

Paul looked straight ahead and said nothing.

"What's the matter? Aren't you happy for them? But it will be marvellous, don't worry."

"I know it will. I'm just a bit sad, that's all."

Jacinthe stopped and turned to look at him.

"You little romantic you! You're fond of them, aren't you?"

"Yes. They're good young people, part of the future of the village."

"Well, I'm sure they'll return after they've made their fortune in Canada. But let's forget them. Let's talk about us, *chéri.* Are you going to apply for a post in Bordeaux soon?"

"Yes, of course. I promise. But I'll have to wait for a GP position to come available before I can do it."

"Let's hope it happens soon. I can't wait for us to be together and I'm hoping my transfer to Bordeaux will come through in few weeks."

Paul held her close to him in reply.

*

Marie came out of the hotel feeling excited. She wanted to see everything in this big city she had dreamed about for so long. Immediately.

But she remained standing on the pavement without moving, amazed by the extraordinary spectacle before her in the street – so many motorcars, horses and carriages. So many people rushing past each other to get to their destination as quickly as possible. Above all she was astonished at the level of noise. She had never seen so much activity on the streets of Gornac or Sauveterre even on market days. Then, to her astonishment she saw a little train coming towards her.

"Alain, what's that? It's a train, but what's it doing in the street!"

"It's called a tramway. Do you want a ride?"

"Can we really? Yes, please. Super!"

Alain signalled to the driver at the tram stop and they climbed aboard. The tram went down the cours de l'Intendance, crossed the place du Grand Théâtre, where it stopped to pick up more passengers, and continued on to the place des Quinconces.

Marvelling, Marie gazed out of the window at all the hustle and bustle in the street. She looked with wonder at the tall buildings on either side of the main street and was impressed by the size of the Grand Théâtre dominating the square behind its imposing row of classical columns running the width of the building.

At the next stop just as they were about to leave the tram Marie grabbed Alain's arm in fright. She whispered:

"Over there! Can you see him? It's Léonce Beynard. Alain, I'm afraid."

He looked in the direction she was pointing.

"No, my sweet. Relax. That's not him. Forget Beynard. Come on, we must get off the tram. We'll walk across the square and down to the quayside by the river. You'll be amazed at what's going on there."

She continued to look anxiously towards the man who looked so like her accuser as Alain helped her down, but the man was moving away from them and was soon lost amongst the crowd. Somewhat reassured she took Alain's arm and let herself be guided across the wide square towards two tall decorated columns on either side of a flight of steps leading down to the quayside.

They paused for a moment at the top of the steps. The scene below her took her breath away. All along the riverbank right up to the Pont de pierre with its seventeen arches and impressive street-lamps, there were all manner of boats, local *gabarres*, barges and even passenger ships. Several boats were attached to the quay, reached only by rough narrow gangplanks which looked to her to be quite unstable. Their sails were furled and loosely rolled round the masts, but were still flapping in the wind off the water.

On the quayside itself there were carts loaded with sacks of grain and flour, bales of hay or piles of logs and with all manner of other goods. The dray horses waited patiently for their masters to unload the goods onto the quay or load them directly onto the waiting boats. Porters pushed or pulled tumbrels and hand-carts, which reminded Marie of the Caïffa carts which Alain had towed with his bicycle past her house in the mornings.

"Look, Alain. That cart there, it looks like the one you used to pull in the village. You didn't know that every morning I watched you go by from my bedroom window, did you? I longed for you to look up, but you never did!"

"Says you! Of course I knew you were watching me, but I wanted to make you fall madly in love with me, so I pretended not to notice. And, as you know, it worked," he added, pulling her towards him to give her a kiss.

Marie pushed him away:

"No, you cheat! If I'd known you were so devious ... "

"What? You wouldn't have married me?"

"Absolutely not! But I didn't know at the time so ... "

Alain quickly stole his kiss and pointed out a boat on the quayside.

"Look over there. Near to the bridge. That *gabarre* loaded with barrels of wine. I recognise it. It's come down the river from La Réole or perhaps even further upstream. The dealer here will unload the wine and stock it in his warehouse by the quay."

He pointed to the buildings all along the waterfront.

"Do you know how the *gabarres* will go back upstream against the current?"

"They'll wait for the tide?"

"No, it doesn't go far enough up the river. They'll dismantle the boat and load the planks and sails onto an ox-cart and go home by road!"

"Really? That's amazing."

"Oh! Look. There's Dr Lasserre."

"*Bonjour, Monsieur le docteur,*" said Alain. "*Je vous présente ma femme, Madame Marie Duvigneau!*"

"*Bonjour, Monsieur Duvigneau. Bonjour, Madame Duvigneau. Enchanté.*"

The little pantomime over, they embraced each other happily. When they were settled in a bistro near the quayside, Alain and Marie immediately wanted to know the latest news from Gornac.

"But you only left yesterday," replied the doctor with a smile. "Are you missing it so much already?"

"No," replied Alain, "but I'm curious all the same. What's the reaction in the village to our wedding? And how is *maman*?"

"I can't tell you much about the villagers' reaction. Some are sorry you have left and others are relieved the whole business is over and life in the village can get back to normal so to speak."

"And what about *maman*?"

"As you can imagine she's sad to see you go, but proud of both of you for being so courageous. As we all are."

"That's nice of you to say that, *Monsieur le docteur*," said Marie.

"You are welcome, Madame Duvigneau. But please call me Paul. You are a married woman now!"

"I wouldn't dare, *Monsieur le docteur.*"

She hesitated.

"Perhaps, on one condition."

"What condition?"

"That you continue to call me Marie and not Madame Duvigneau!"

"Agreed! So let's get down to serious business. Coffee for you both or something stronger?"

"Coffee for me, Paul," replied Alain.

Marie nodded not quite daring to use his first name.

Paul signalled to the waiter to bring them three coffees.

"Firstly, congratulations again on your wedding."

"Thank you, Paul, that's kind," said Marie blushing. "It's partly thanks to you of course that we are married."

"But now explain to me what you are going to do in Québec. I have to admit I'm a bit jealous. It will be a great adventure for you both and I think you are very courageous to go."

"Frankly Paul, we don't know exactly! The cousins are going to look after us at first. My great uncle André has told me he has kept a job open for me in his pulp mill. It will be hard physical work, I think, but I'm used to manual work in the vineyard."

"And they've found us a house to rent," continued Marie. "So I'll be busy making the house habitable. I'll have to learn quickly how to buy food and things for the house."

"You're not afraid of the winter?" asked Paul. "They say the winters are long and very cold."

"We'll learn how to cope with the winter from our cousins and we'll have the whole summer to prepare," said Alain with a grin. "You're asking the same questions as my mother and Madame Marceau did!"

"You're right. I'm behaving like a worried parent, but it's because I'm fond of you both. I know you're going to manage very well and I wish you all the happiness possible. I'm going to miss you two young things!"

"Thank you, *Monsieur le docteur* ... Paul! Without you and Madame Lucette I'd still be a maid of all work, which is the same as good for nothing and with no job."

"Not at all. We would have found another solution, Marie. But luckily there was Alain! Now tell me your immediate plans."

"We're going to spend another day here in Bordeaux. Then we'll take the train to Paris and spend a few days days there. Finally we'll travel to Cherbourg to wait for the arrival of the liner from England which will take us to Québec."

"What a fabulous itinerary. Have you ever seen the sea, Marie? Nor you, Alain?"

"No," they replied together.

"How fantastic to see the sea for the first time. I love the sea, but my work stops me from going to the coast as much as I'd like. One of the advantages of Jacinthe working in Biarritz is that I have a good excuse to go and see the ocean. And her of course!

"Right. Enough questions," he said, getting to his feet. "I shall leave you in peace. Jacinthe is here in Bordeaux today and we're meeting for lunch. Have a wonderful trip and I wish you every good fortune for your new life in Québec."

The three of them stood up and embraced. Before he left Paul looked at Marie.

"I'm not going to give up finding out the truth about the jewels, Marie, I promise you."

Marie hugged him again, tears in her eyes before catching Alain up and taking his arm. After a few steps they turned round and saw the doctor watching them go with sadness in his eyes. Marie waved before the two of turned away for the final time.

"I'll miss Paul, you know," she said. "He always supported me long before the business with the jewels. He knew Madame Coustaut was a difficult woman and he did all he could to improve my working conditions. He even insisted she give me time off."

"We'll keep in touch with him and with Madame Marceau as well as the family of course. We can write to them often and in time we'll perhaps have a telephone."

"It was so difficult to call him Paul! I was embarrassed. He's so kind. I hope he'll be able to marry his fiancée soon. Have you met Jacinthe, Alain?"

"No, but whenever he came to the house to see my parents, he often talked about her."

They continued to walk along the waterfront so occupied by their thoughts that this time they hardly noticed all the activity and noise around them.

Alain turned into the street leading to the place du vieux Parlement looking for a restaurant where they could have lunch.

"Did you never have any idea where Madame Coustaut could have hidden the jewels?"

"No, none at all. I'd no idea they even existed. But ever since I've wondered whether Monsieur might have sold them."

"I don't think so. He hated working at the windmill. He felt humiliated. So, if he had had any money, he would have stopped working for Monsieur Serizier, I'm sure."

"You're right. It'll always remain a mystery."

They chose a restaurant and Alain ordered the set menu for them both. Sitting outside on the terrasse they soaked up the soft warmth of the April sun. Their conversation turned to their plans for their future in Québec.

"Alain, I'm afraid of this voyage in the liner," she said. "It's so far and the journey is so long. Six days! And these liners are dangerous. You do know that a huge English liner sank in the middle of the ocean near Canada and hundreds of people were drowned?"

"You talking about the Titanic! Don't worry, my sweet. They say was the captain's fault for not paying attention to the warnings he received of icebergs in the area. There shouldn't be any icebergs when we cross and that happened fifteen years ago. Communications have improved since then."

"I just hope you're right! But tell me about Paris. Will this be the first time for you too?"

"Not quite. I went there with my father to the Salon des Vins in 1920, but I was fifteen and I don't remember much about it. But Paris is big – bigger than Bordeaux – and very beautiful. We're going to have a great time."

"Super! I'm hungry. Ah, here's our waiter."

The waiter arrived with their first course.

"You know, Alain, all my life I have watched other people eat. When I was in the village in Gornac I could see people eating in the restaurants or in the Grand Hôtel. Today is the first time I have been served instead of serving."

Despite himself Alain felt emotional at her words and reached over to squeeze her arm.

"Now you are my wife, this will not be the last time I promise you."

It was turning cold in the late afternoon and they decided to go back to the hotel. There were few people in the streets now and the shops weren't open on a Sunday, but Marie couldn't resist doing some window-shopping. On the cours de L'Intendence she stood admiring the dresses in the window displays of the fashion boutiques. For the young woman who had never been able to afford such luxury the dresses seemed like the sort you would see in fashion magazines but which didn't exist in real life.

Alain was conscious of her astonishment and her wish to wear dresses like those which so bedazzled her. She turned to him as if reading his thoughts.

"Don't worry, my darling. These dresses are pretty, very sweet, but not at all practical. I can't see myself wearing dresses like that in the Québecois countryside! Or even in the town. These are party clothes.

"In Chicoutimi there will be shops where we'll be able to buy ourselves really warm practical clothes for the winter. I wouldn't survive in these flimsy dresses!"

"You're right, my sweet, but one day I'm going to buy you the dresses of your dreams, I promise."

Marie tore herself away from the shop windows and they continued up the street holding hands.

"Tomorrow we must go to the Hôtel de Ville. We have to get your new passport. *Papa* has seen to everything and when we hand them our marriage certificate they'll give you your passport in the name of Madame Marie Duvigneau."

Looking round to see who was watching she pulled him close and kissed him

Chapter 14

Wednesday, 18th April 1928

Bernard Duvigneau was working in his office when he heard a knock on the door. He got up to answer it and was delighted to see Paul Lasserre standing there.

"Come in Paul. How good to see you," he said. "Not busy this morning then?"

"Bonjour, Bernard," he replied shaking his hand. "No, no home visits today. In the spring fewer people complain about feeling ill!"

"Excellent. Come in and sit down. Coffee? Or perhaps something stronger?"

"Coffee, please. Alcohol on my breath when I'm examining patients is not good for my reputation!"

"Your reputation is impeccable, my dear friend. Come into the kitchen and I can make the coffee while you tell me what you are up to at the moment."

Paul sat at the table in the kitchen and watched Bernard as he switched on the cafetière and looked for the cups.

"I bumped into Alain and Marie by chance on the waterfront in Bordeaux on Sunday. We spent a pleasant few minutes together."

"Excellent. How were they?"

"Excited. A little nervous perhaps. Especially Marie."

"It's a huge change for her, but she has a strong temperament and will manage alright."

"True. But at first it won't be easy. Luckily spring is coming, but it will be hard in the long winter."

"Yes, but the cousins are used it over there. They know how to cope and will help Alain and Marie to prepare."

"You're right again! Alain even accused me of asking the same worried parent-type questions as Simone and Lucette did!"

"That's my boy! He loves to joke."

"He said your uncle André has kept a job open for him in his pulp mill?"

"Yes. André confirmed it in a letter which arrived just before their wedding. The pulp mill belongs to the family. That will give them time to decide what they really want to do."

"Does it take a long time for letters to arrive?"

"Two or three weeks. It depends on the liners. I thought of contacting André in Chicoutimi by this new radio telephone which Alain mentioned. But it costs a thousand francs for three minutes! Just not possible. No, we'll wait for the letters."

"They must be in Paris now, I think?"

"Yes. They have a few days to explore the capital before going to Cherbourg. The liner leaves on May 4th. "

"How is Simone?"

"Oh! You know. Women always fuss over the youngest. She'll miss him. Me too. He always had lots of energy and enthusiasm, but also common sense, a practical side and good ideas."

"He still has, Bernard! I can see you miss him already."

"Yes, I do."

"You know I won't give up trying to find out the truth about the jewels, don't you? One day I'll find the answer and they'll be able to return if they wish."

"Thank you, Paul. We're grateful for all you've done. I just hope they won't have any difficulties boarding the Ausonia in Cherbourg," Bernard added.

"What do you mean?"

"There was a pile of official paperwork to go through to prepare for their departure. Luckily we were able to do it all in the Hôtel de Ville in Bordeaux. Québec imposes many restrictions on immigration."

"But since they have family there and are French … "

"True, but obtaining a passport for Marie was not easy as her parents are dead and she was not yet married. I had to act as Guarantor, but in the end it worked out."

"Don't worry, Bernard. It will all be fine."

Chapter 15

Thursday, 3rd May 1928

The ten days they spent in Paris had flashed by. They had visited 'everything'. Alain telephoned his parents to tell them what they were doing and Marie was able to speak to Lucette who went to the Duvigneau house to take the call.

During the visit both of them, but especially Marie, had grown in confidence. Surrounded by so many people in the city and absorbing so many new experiences and ideas, the visit served as training and preparation for the voyage to come and for the move to Chicoutimi with all the demands which would be made on them.

On the morning of May 3rd they boarded the Train Atlantique Express for Cherbourg at the St-Lazarre-Maintes-la-Jolie station. The saloon-type carriages were much more luxurious than the carriages on the line from St Brice to Bordeaux-Passerelles. They were impressed by the comfort which resembled more the inside of a hotel lounge than a railway carriage, and particularly by the buffet car where they could have lunch during the journey just as if they were in a fine restaurant.

Five hours later they took a taxi to their hotel. From the window of their room Marie stood looking out at the sea, stunned at the spectacular sight of the vastness of the ocean.

"Alain, come and look. It's amazing. The ocean. It's enormous."

"You're right," he said, standing beside her at the window. "It's the first time I've seen it too. Do you want to go and walk along the beach by the water?"

"Can we? But of course!"

"Let's go then. Bring your coat. The wind will be cold."

At first they walked gingerly on the pebbly sand. Then with the wind in their faces, together they ran along the beach laughing and jumping with pleasure like young children.

They stopped, out of breath, and Marie took off her shoes.

"What are you doing?"

"I want to walk in the water. Just on the edge, of course."

"Mind the stones, they'll hurt your feet," he said, his words blown away by the wind. But Marie had already run to the edge of the sea and was paddling bare-footed in the freezing water. Every now and then she squealed when she tripped on a rock or walked on a sharp stone. Alain was over the moon to see her so happy.

They went back to the hotel tired but delighted with their afternoon. In their room Marie looked out of the window. On the horizon a black speck was growing larger as she watched. She kept staring at it, fascinated, until she realised it was a liner.

"Alain, come quickly! Over there on the horizon. Is that our ship?"

Alain looked for a moment as the liner rapidly grew larger and was clearly heading for the port.

"Yes, that's the Ausonia coming from England, from Southampton. It's our magic carpet to transport us to Québec."

"Don't be silly, it's just a ship! It's huge. As big as a hotel."

She turned towards him.

"Are we really going to spend six days on board? Does it have bedrooms? What about restaurants? How are we going to eat? Do they speak French on board? How are we going to manage? We don't speak English."

"So many questions! Yes, there are bedrooms, called cabins. We are going to eat, or dine, in the restaurant or dining room and I'm sure they speak French on board. But I can speak a bit of English."

"I didn't know that," she said, impressed. "We must pack quickly before it leaves," she added, rushing to the wardrobe.

"Slow down, my sweet. It's not like a bus. The ship won't leave before 1500 hours tomorrow afternoon. We will have to go down to the port tomorrow morning to go through customs and go on board."

He looked out of the window and saw that the Ausonia was preparing to come alongside the dock.

"This evening I'll order something to eat to be brought up to our room."

Marie wasn't listening. She was too busy packing.

Chapter 16

Friday, 4ᵗʰ May 1928

The next morning Alain leafed through the documents his father had given him to find the number of their cabin on board. He attached a label to each piece of luggage and rang the reception desk to arrange for a taxi to take them and their luggage down to the port. They were due to present themselves at the embarkation point at eleven o'clock to complete the formalities.

Despite himself he felt nervous. He was leaving France. When would he return, he wondered? Not wanting to communicate his nervousness to Marie, he busied himself putting the luggage outside the door of their room, but he couldn't stop asking himself if they had made the right decision. After two weeks away from the village and after all they had seen and done in Bordeaux and Paris, he wondered if they hadn't exaggerated the animosity of the villagers towards Marie. Perhaps they should have faced everyone down and stayed in the village. He was really going to miss his family, but he knew too they were starting a great adventure and would be able to return home in a few years with the money they had saved.

He continued to debate with himself back and forth until the porter knocked on the door to take their luggage.

*

"Do you still believe those jewels ever existed, Paul?" asked Bernard. "You don't think they were just a simple figment of Léonce's imagination?"

"No, I'm sure they do, since he continues to search desperately for them. He said he saw them when he was a little boy. All I can think of is that their mother hid them and didn't reveal the hiding place to Élise before she died."

"So unless he completely destroys the house we're not going to find them!"

"Just be patient! That's exactly what Léonce is doing!"

"What does Lucette think? I'm sure she would like to sell the house."

"True, but she can't sell it without the agreement of her brother."

"Do you think she believes in these jewels?"

"Difficult to say. She was very young when Léonce said their mother showed them to them, but she has a vague memory that what he says is true. So, the mystery goes on."

"For Marie's sake, I hope it's soon solved. Another coffee, Paul?"

*

At the embarkation point Alain and Marie were waiting patiently in the long queue to show their passports and documents. There were mixed feelings amongst the people waiting with them. Some were excited at the prospect of the adventure they were starting, others waited silently trying to control their feelings of worry and sadness.

Finally they reached the head of the queue and went out onto the quayside. The liner seemed even bigger now they were so close. Its flanks towered above them and cast a shadow on the line of passengers who were climbing aboard, often with some difficulty, up the steep gangway.

Marie hesitated for a moment like many in front of her before starting up the gangway, realising she was leaving French soil perhaps for good.

"It's OK, it's OK," Alain encouraged her. "We can come back to see the family as often as you want."

"Are you sure, Alain? I don't want to think I'll never again see our little village and your family who are mine too now."

"Yes, I'm sure. Now go! Climb up!"

"What's the number of our cabin?"

"23."

"That's the same number as our house in Gonin! So we will be in my home on board," she said, attempting a smile.

Cabin number 23 was quite comfortably set up: two bunk beds, a sofa, a wardrobe and a dressing table.

"It's not exactly a hotel, but not too bad," said Alain. "For the lavatory we have to go down the corridor."

"It's a pity there's no window, but like you say, not too bad," said Marie, testing out the mattress suspiciously.

"I can see you've become used to the luxury of hotel bedrooms, my sweet. Reality will not be long in coming!"

"But we will have a house in Chicoutimi, won't we Alain?"

"Yes, but don't go imagining too much luxury, especially at the beginning when we arrive. The houses are built of wood and I don't know if there'll be much furniture."

"Well, we'll see … ," she was saying as someone knocked at the cabin door.

Alain went to open it. It was the porter with their bags.

"Thank you," he said, handing him a ten franc note.

"Let's leave all that for later," she said, looking at the pile of cases. "I want to explore the ship and watch the departure from the outside deck."

She pushed him out of the door.

*

At home Lucette was preparing lunch. She was expecting Francis and Eugénie. Despite the pleasure she always felt whenever her son and daughter-in-law came to visit, she was sad. She knew that today was the day Marie and Alain would leave French soil and that she might not ever see them again.

The whole affair of the stolen jewels concocted by her brother had led to them leaving the village. On the one hand she knew it was a fabulous opportunity for the young couple, but at the same time what a shambles it had caused! The village was divided into two opposing camps and she feared the rancour would last a long time. People don't forgive and forget easily; the bad feeling would be passed from generation to generation.

"No, no," she said aloud. "Don't be so silly. You're letting your feelings run riot. It will all be quickly forgotten and life in the village will return to normal."

The kitchen door opened and Alain came in smiling.

"Have you started talking to yourself, *maman*?" he said kissing her on both cheeks.

"No! Yes! I was thinking of Marie and Alain. You realise it's today they leave?"

She stopped as she saw Eugénie enter the kitchen behind him.

"Bonjour, Eugénie. How are you? You look blooming today."

"Thank you, Grandma. That's kind."

"Grandma? Is that your way of telling me you're expecting a baby?" she exclaimed, putting her arms around her and giving her a hug. "I'm so happy for the two of you. Come in. Sit down. Are you well? Not too tired?"

"*Maman*, enough! Eugénie is not ill. You've just said she looks blooming. Paul says she's in excellent health."

"When are you due?" asked Lucette, smiling happily.

"At the end of November, mother-in-law. A lovely Christmas present."

"Do you want a boy or a girl?"

"It doesn't matter. Just a healthy baby, that's all," Eugénie replied.

"We must celebrate! Francis, go and fetch a special bottle of wine from the cellar."

He left the kitchen and taking advantage of his absence Lucette asked more intimate questions of her daughter-in-law.

"No, really I'm fine. No problems. Some morning sickness but nothing serious."

"Good. Lucky you, Eugénie. My morning sickness was terrible when I was expecting Francis. Your mother must be so pleased?"

"Yes, she's delighted. Such a shame *papa* is no longer here," she replied.

"Yes, and my husband too. That terrible war. No, no, don't apologise. Let's forget all that. Ah! Francis! What have you chosen? A *vin de garage* from Domaine le Frègne. Bernard Duvigneau would be pleased with your choice. We will drink the health of Marie and Alain too.

"Go and sit down, children. It's all ready."

*

On the promenade deck of the Ausonia Alain and Marie were leaning against the railings. The liner was tied up against the quay in the outer harbour. They could see across to the Napoleonic dockyard where the ship builders were working.

"See over there, my sweet. In 1853 Napoleon III came to open what they call the Second Arsenal. At the same time he opened the new train line from Cherbourg to Paris which we have just travelled on."

Marie hardly reacted. She was remembering her life in Gornac and thinking of her mother and father.

"The Emperor even invited Queen Victoria and Prince Albert of England to come and see the Arsenal. There were huge celebrations to mark the visit," he continued, still without arousing Marie's interest.

"Alain, I'm sorry but at the moment I feel so sad and full of longing for our village. I'm wondering how your parents are and Madame Lucette and Francis and Eugénie. I miss them so much already."

"I do too, but we're beginning an amazing adventure and as I said we can come back in a few years to see the family. Québec is not at the end of the world. Just a week's journey away. That's all."

"You're right. I'm being silly."

Suddenly a loud blast on the ship's siren echoed around the harbour signalling the ship's departure.

"Look, those men on the quay are throwing off the mooring lines. We're off!"

The liner was already moving away from the quayside with the help of a tug. Those on the quayside were waving to friends and families on board, waving hats, handkerchiefs and umbrellas.

Marie watched them, sad there was no-one on the quay to wave her and Alain off.

Turning to him she said, with tears in her eyes:

"I've seen enough. Let's go back to the cabin to unpack. And I'm hungry. We must find out where the restaurant is."

*

When the meal was over Francis helped his mother in the kitchen with the washing up. Eugénie was resting in the living room. Now was a good time for a conversation with his mother about his aunt Élise's house.

"*Maman*, I know Uncle Léonce is convinced the jewels exist, but what do you think?"

"I think so too, but I don't know if they are still in the house. It's simply impossible to think Élise could have sold them, but it is possible our mother hid them or put them in a safe place without revealing where to my sister. Frankly she was not well towards the end of her life. She didn't even recognise us when we went to see her, so there is no way she could have told us about the jewels and where she had hidden them."

"So Uncle Léonce is probably right?"

"Yes, but what good is that? We've searched everywhere. But Léonce will demolish the house rather than give up trying to find them. The house is worth as much as the jewels I'm sure."

"We must persuade him to sell it then. Do you want me to ...."

"Definitely not! He has to convince himself the jewels are no longer there. Don't worry, we will sell the house one day, my son. We just have to be patient."

Chapter 17

Saturday, 5th May 1928

The next morning Alain and Marie made their way to the ship's dining room for breakfast. They hadn't slept well. The movement of the boat had disturbed them for most of the night, but fortunately neither of them suffered from sea sickness and now they were hungry.

Surprised by the variety of food on offer, they refused the traditional English bacon and eggs and just chose brioches and coffee. Sitting at a table for two they looked out of the porthole. The ship was approaching a harbour on the west coast of Ireland. It was raining and dark clouds scudded across a grey menacing sky.

"So this is Queenstown. It's in Ireland," Alain said to himself, remembering his father's words.

"It looks so dismal."

"True, it's not pretty in the rain. But look at the church. That's impressive how it dominates the port and the houses."

"But it's all so grey and sad. I miss the sun and blue skies of Aquitaine."

"Well, we're not staying here long. Just enough time to let the new passengers board before we leave for Québec."

"We've another five days at sea, haven't we?"

"Yes. Uncle André and his family will be in Québec City to welcome us and to take us to Chicoutimi."

"Tell me more about these cousins. Who are they again?I keep forgetting."

"André is the son of my great-uncle, my grandfather's brother, who left France for Québec at the end of the last century, so about forty years ago. My father has always kept in touch with his uncles and cousins. They settled in Chicoutimi. It's a small town by a river where they started a pulp mill."

"What is a pulp mill exactly?"

"I'm not completely sure, but I think it's like a saw mill, but instead of producing planks they grind the timber into wood pulp. Uncle André will explain it all to us."

"Right, let's get our coats. I want to go out onto the deck to see the new passengers."

From high up on the deck they watched the emigrants coming on board the ship. They looked sad and downtrodden. The recent civil war in Ireland had exhausted the country. These people were all seeking a new life in North America.

With the arrival of the new passengers the atmosphere on board changed completely. Irish voices were heard everywhere and the sound of Irish fiddles, songs and folk dancing echoed throughout the ship. Some passengers complained, but Marie understood it was their way of maintaining their traditions, of not forgetting their origins and of keeping up their morale. They had lost so much. To take away their identity would mean total defeat for them.

Marie and Alain spent the remainder of the voyage in a simple routine. Eat, sleep, read in the cabin, walk the decks when the weather allowed, gaze at the unchanging horizon and think of France.

They didn't have much contact with the other passengers. The majority didn't speak French and their accent when speaking English was so strong that Alain, who was proud of being able to speak and understand English, gave up completely when faced with the Irish in particular. As for the French passengers who had joined the ship like them in

Cherbourg, they were hardly to be seen. Most of them were laid low by sea sickness.

Chapter 18

Thursday, 10th May 1928

They woke up after another bad night due to the violent tossing of the ship. Alain started to get dressed but the liner was rolling and pitching so much he found it difficult to stand upright. Several times he was thrown against the sides of the cabin.

"What's happening, Alain? I'm scared," asked Marie, who was prudently staying in her bunk. There was not enough room in such sea conditions for both of them to get up at the same time in the narrow cabin.

"The weather has worsened and we must be in the midst of a storm. Wait here while I go and look out of the portholes in the restaurant. It's impossible to see anything from here."

"Be careful and don't go out on deck! Please, Alain!"

"Promise."

Alain left the cabin and struggled to keep his balance as he went along the corridor to the companionway which led to the upper decks and to the restaurants. The corridor smelled of vomit. Grabbing every hand hold he could he managed to reach the stairs and went up to the restaurant. It was deserted except for the waiters. They were ready to serve breakfast but there were no customers. He approached the counter.

« Good morning. What would you like, sir ? » asked the waiter with a smile.

« *Bonjour.* No, thank you. What happens ? » he asked, embarrassed into stuttering his English.

« We are in the Gulf of the Saint Lawrence. It's always rough here, sir » the waiter replied.

« *Merci, monsieur,* » said Alain, going over to the porthole.

Through the spray and the enormous white capped waves stretching away on all sides he briefly made out land. The ship was entering the mouth of the Saint-Laurent river, but the estuary was so wide he could not see both banks at the same time. There were even still some patches of floating pack-ice being tossed on the waves and he could hear them breaking apart as they crashed against the sides of the ship. He shivered despite the warmth inside the dining room.

He went back down to the cabin to fetch Marie. She had managed to get dressed and was ready to go out.

"The sea will calm down soon. We're in the mouth of the Saint-Laurent and the waves are quite high. The river is so wide that it still looks like the ocean. I can't see both banks."

"We're almost there then."

"Yes, but we won't arrive before tomorrow evening. There is still roughly a thousand kilometres to go from the mouth to reach Québec City."

"A thousand kilometres! In a river? It's enormous! How far is it from Bordeaux to Paris?"

"600 or 700 kilometres, I think."

"So further than that! *Incroyable!*"

"Come on, let's go and eat. There's no-one in the restaurant, so no queues."

"Good. I'm hungry and I've had enough of this cabin. I can't wait to get to land. I'm not cut out to be a sailor!"

"Me neither, frankly. Let's eat and then perhaps we will be able to see the coast."

During the day the estuary gradually narrowed and they could just make out both banks. The waves became more regular and they were able to go out onto the upper deck.

On both sides the banks were covered in dense forests of tall firs. Often the trees came right down to the edge of the water. Here and there in small clearings they could see log cabins and clouds of smoke rising from the chimneys only to be blown away by the wind. The land in most places was still covered in snow and the trees on the higher ground had not lost their snowy caps.

"It's so cold!" exclaimed Marie, pulling her coat more tightly around her. "Look, there's ice on the river. But it's May! When does spring come in this country?"

"Soon, my sweet. It will be hot this summer, you'll see."

"Look over there. That lighthouse is huge."

"I think we're going to stop there. It's called Pointe-au-Père."

"Funny name. Why are we going to stop?"

"There will be an medical inspection of those in third class. For us in the cabins there won't be a problem. We'll be continuing to Québec quite soon."

Fortunately there were no medical problems amongst the passengers and the Ausonia left Pointe-au-Père with little delay. The ship passed by Grosse Île, a former quarantine station, and at last they could see Québec City. The lights of the town became more and more spectacular against the evening sky as they approached. The silhouette of the Château de Frontenac took their breath away.

"Look Alain. The château is all lit up. Even in Paris that would be magnificent. It's as big as the Louvre or the Palais Royal," she said, proud of being able to show off her knowledge of the capital.

"So now you can see this is a great civilised country, just like France. We won't feel at all far from home."

The ship moored up in the Princess Louise harbour. It was late and everyone would spend one more night aboard before disembarking.

Chapter 19

Friday, 11th May 1928

The next day was sunny but the cold was fierce. First class and cabin passengers were offered breakfast on board before disembarking with their luggage. Third class were already on the quayside.

In the dining room Marie was feeling nervous and had no appetite for breakfast.

"What's going to happen now, Alain?"

"There will be a medical examination; they'll inspect our documents and ask about the amount of money we're bringing in. Since we're coming to join family there'll be no problem."

"Will we be together?"

"No, I don't think so. But don't worry. Just answer their questions and it will all be fine. You've got your new passport? Just remember you are married and your name is Marie Duvigneau!"

After breakfast all the remaining passengers went to fetch their cases from their cabins and queued on the deck to go down the steep gang-plank. Once they were on the Princess Louise Quay, they were guided to the Immigrants' Building where the formalities began for entering Canada.

*

In Gornac, spring was proving to be mild after the cold winter. The buds on the vines were already opening and those working in the fields could feel the warmth of the sun on their backs. There was no more fear of a late frost.

At Domaine Le Frègne Bernard Duvigneau and his sons were directing the work of a group of journeymen as they did each year. Alain's two older brothers missed the presence of their younger brother who always had a smile on his lips and an easy laugh. Married for several years already they had liked watching him, feeling slightly jealous if they were honest, chase after the girls in the village. But they had noticed he often went to walk on the hill in Gonin without giving any convincing reason. They soon realised that he had set his heart on a young girl called Marie Bourdet who lived close to the three windmills.

At the time they had teased him over his choice, but they knew she was an honest and respectable young woman and, despite what happened later, they were happy for both of them when they wed. Now Alain's brothers were waiting like the rest of the family for news from Québec.

*

In Gonin, Lucette went to help her daughter-in-law whenever Francis had to go away for a few days on business. The idea of becoming a grandmother before the end of the year gave her great joy. But during the weeks Marie had stayed with her after her father died, Lucette had enjoyed having another woman in the house and treated Marie as she would have treated her daughter. The two of them had become close.

Lucette wondered constantly how she and Alain would manage in Québec, a country she herself could not in any way picture in her mind. Was it like the Entre-deux-mers region of her birth or even the like the Landes further to the south with all its pine trees, she wondered. Were there really savage Redskins like it said in the books? What were the French in Québec like? She had heard they still spoke like people did in seventeenth century France, but she had no idea what that would sound like.

*

Paul Lasserre too often thought of the young couple. When they had met in Bordeaux – already a month ago – the two young people were so happy to be together, but he had sensed their nervousness about what was ahead of them. He still wondered if his idea that they should leave the village and emigrate to Canada was as well founded as he had thought at the time. Was it a suggestion made too soon in the heat of the crisis, so to speak? Would the suspicions, the mistrust even, of the villagers towards Marie have waned after a few weeks, especially after her father died?

Had he acted too quickly to protect her? He was conscious there were others in the village who were also asking themselves if they had judged Marie too quickly and too harshly. The disappearance of two young adults so full of life had made an impression on people's minds and they were beginning to feel their absence. In a small village young people with their energy and new ideas represented the future of the community, a new start after the hardships following the Grande Guerre. Now they were gone.

Paul was waiting anxiously like everyone else for news of the young couple.

Chapter 20

Monday, 9th July 1928

"Bernard! Come quickly! There's a letter from Alain and Marie," shouted Simone.

She had snatched the letter out of the hands of the postman who was as excited as she was and burning to have news of the young couple for whom he had great affection. But Simone, too preoccupied to notice, had thanked him and closed the door leaving him none the wiser on the doorstep.

She ran into the living room calling to her husband again. Bernard came in trying to wake himself up after a bad night. He kissed his wife and they sat together on the sofa. Simone nearly ripped the letter, so eager was she to open the envelope, and uttered a sigh of relief on reading the first words. Bernard put his arm round his wife so he could see better and they read it together, commenting on some descriptions and on the winter temperatures.

"You see, my dear," said Bernard, "all is well and our cousins have seen to everything for them."

"You're right. I'm so relieved. I was so worried. It's such a long way away and they are so young."

Suddenly she exclaimed: "Alain hasn't said anything about the Indians or the bears, Bernard. Are they keeping something from us?"

"Simone! Chicoutimi is a proper town, it's not a forest. The Indians are like us. They are hunters and farmers. They've lived there for centuries."

But she wasn't listening and seemed to forget her fears from one moment to the next. She got up quickly from the sofa, a plan forming in her mind.

"We must invite all the family to the house this evening to read them the letter. And Lucette, and Francis and Eugénie, and Paul of course. And the mayor and …. I must go and arrange everything."

"Calm down, Simone," said Bernard, but she had already gone into the kitchen to talk to the cook.

He picked the letter up off the sofa and read it again more slowly.

Chicoutimi, Sunday 17th June 1928

Chers parents,

All is well and I finally have a moment to write to you. I know this letter will take several days or even weeks to reach you in dear old Gornac, so what I write now will no longer be up to date when you receive the letter, but there's nothing I can do about that!

I hope all the family are well: my sisters and brothers-in-law, my brothers and sisters-in-law, my nieces and nephews and of course you my dear parents. I wonder if there are any new grandchildren since we left. Say hello to everyone from us and to Paul and Madame Marceau, and Francis and Eugénie as well of course.

We arrived with no problems in Québec City. The crossing was long but our cabin was quite comfortable – thanks, papa – and when the sea wasn't too rough we were able to go on the outside decks and get some fresh air. Frankly there wasn't much to see. The ocean was covered in white sheep as we say, or white horses as the English say – both funny expressions now I think about it – and stretched monotonous and grey out to the horizon all around. We rarely saw another ship.

The first day we docked briefly in Queenstown on the west coast of Ireland to take on more passengers – Irish emigrants. Papa, this Queenstown is in Ireland, not in America!

The Irish speak English, but I couldn't understand a word because their accent is so broad. But they were really nice and loved to sing and dance especially at first. But after the first storm on the third day everyone was sea-sick, except us luckily, and the dancing stopped!

Finally after five days we saw the coast of Terre Neuve and Cap Breton. We entered the estuary of the Saint-Laurent river. It's so big that it took two more days to arrive at Québec City. There were more medical examinations and document checks, but everything went without a hitch. Marie almost forgot her new name, but luckily the customs official just laughed and let her pass!

Here all is well. The Tremblay family welcomed us warmly and we have spent hours describing our life in Gornac and on drawing family trees of all the family in France. They are as curious to know about our way of life in France as we are to know about theirs!

Uncle André and Aunt Louise have four children – which you know – two sons, Jacques and Étienne and two daughters, Pierrette and Therese. All four are married and they have twelve children between them. We are trying to learn all their names without calling them by the wrong name when we talk to them!

They have found us a house to rent in the town. The houses here are all built of wood. Ours too, of course. On the ground floor there is the living room, dining room and kitchen. The upstairs is under the eaves with three bedrooms and pretty mansard-style windows. It's all very nice and really much too big for the two of us, but all the houses are like this.

Outside along the front of the house is a sort of wooden terrace – a 'deck' – protected by a balustrade. People here sit outside in rocking chairs on the deck when it's warm. In front of the house we have a small fenced-off garden and then there is the road. There is also a back garden where I'll make a vegetable patch when I have time.

We are very happy with the house and the rent is not high. Marie is delighted and has already created a really comfortable home with furniture which people have given us. All the neighbours have lent a hand to help us settle in. We are 'exotic' to them and they want to know everything about us!

Jacques and Étienne have been a great help and their wives, Marguerite and Anne, have taken Marie in hand. She now knows exactly where to go in town to buy food and clothes. We are being really well looked after. I can't thank everyone enough. Everyone tells us we must have everything set up before the end of August so that we are ready for winter. Summers are short here and even September can be cold.

When we arrived last month it was still cold and we had to buy coats, parkas they call them here. Actually we are learning all sorts of new words and expressions. It's French but with a strong accent, a bit like the accent at home of people who still speak patois or gascon. We often have to ask people to repeat things they say. Marie understands better than I do.

The family told us that this past year was very hard with lots of snow. It went down to minus 30 and even to minus 40! I hope we are going to be able to heat the house well next winter.

At the moment however it never seems to stop pouring with rain. There is a large lake called Lac Saint Jean north of here up the river Saguenay. The villages around it have been badly flooded and people have had to be evacuated. They have really strange names – Sainte Méthode, Roberval, Peribonka.

People tell us there has been a huge scandal over the cause of these floods and the recent construction of dams in the area, but we don't know much about it yet. Jacques has promised to tell us the story sometime.

I'm going to start work at the pulp mill tomorrow. Jacques will come with me and explain how it all works. I admit I'm a bit nervous about what to expect, but it's time I learnt the job and earned some money. The holiday's over!

So there you are. That's all for the moment. Marie sends her love to everyone and asks if you will show this letter to Madame Marceau, please.

Your loving son

Alain

Chapter 21

Friday, 5ᵗʰ October 1928

At the vineyard Bernard and his sons were busy with the work which needed to be done now that all the grapes were in. The harvest had been quick that year. The grapes were of good quality and for once the presses had operated without a hitch throughout the three weeks of the picking. Now the vats were full to the brim.

They had to work fast with the white wine – the main crop – and separate the pressed grapes quickly from the solids and impurities. For the red the maceration in the oak barrels would last a few more days before the juice was drained off and the solid residue pressed a second time.

The three of them were talking together and sampling a glass of the first pressing of the white wine – the *'bourru'* – when the postman knocked and entered the winery.

"Hello, Bernard. Hello lads," he said, waving a letter in front of him. "Here's a letter you've been waiting for."

He handed the envelope to Bernard who thanked him and looked at the Canadian stamp.

"It's from Alain. Right, let's go back to the house. I daren't open it without your mother being there!"

*

Paul took a few days leave and went to Hosségor to see Jacinthe. It was a beautiful day and they had decided to spend the day in Biarritz, where they walked along the beach, well wrapped up against the cold breeze off the sea.

"Have you had any more news of that young couple who emigrated to Canada? Marie and Alain?" asked Jacinthe. "Have their parents received any more letters?"

"Not that I know of. It often takes weeks for letters to arrive."

"Yes, I know, but I'm curious to know more about life in Québec and what the French there are like. And I'd love to know more about how the native peoples live."

"Me too. We'll just have to wait for the next letter. It won't be long I'm sure."

They continued to walk along the sand until they reached the steps up to the bridge which linked a small rocky island to the shore. There were few people about that October Friday and they were alone when they reached the harbour on the far side.

"I think I can ask to be transferred to Bordeaux in two years' time. I'm learning so much here at the hospital and I like being by the sea, but I want to be near you even more."

"And I want to be with you," he said, putting his arm around her. "I'll apply for a post in Bordeaux as soon as one comes free, I promise."

"So what shall we do this evening?" she asked.

"I thought we could go for a meal in that good little restaurant in the market hall and then go back to Hosségor."

"So you wish to spend the night with me, *monsieur*?"

"If you are willing, *mademoiselle!*"

She broke free of him and danced backwards ahead of him across the sand, hair flying in the wind, looking teasingly back at him as he followed.

"And what do you propose for tomorrow, *monsieur*?"

"Tomorrow I suggest a road trip to Saint Sebastian. If we leave early we could have lunch in the old town."

"Super! It's a pity we can't spend the weekend there and stay in a hotel."

"You never know, its worth a try. Spain is old fashioned, but it's 1928 after all!"

She let him catch her up and threw her arms around him.

*

Simone made coffee for the three men when they arrived back at the house and they all went into the living room to listen to Bernard read the letter out to them.

Chicoutimi, Sunday 19th August 1928

Chère maman, cher papa,

I finally have a day off to write to you. I have been working now at the pulp mill for four weeks. The work is hard but interesting. The mill is a large building of several storeys right on the banks of the Chicoutimi river which is fast flowing even in the summer. A huge volume of water comes down from Lake Kénogami, which I haven't seen yet, controlled by dams – called discharge basins here – which produce electricity. Jacques told me that before the construction of the first dam, in 1912 at Pont-Gustave, everything was run by water power just like our water mills at home.

Our wood for the mill arrives by river, but not on barges! The firs and spruce are felled, stripped of their branches and topped off. Then the logs are hauled by horses or tractors to the riverside. There they are thrown into the river and come down on the current like our gabarres on the Garonne. Where the river is wide enough they are lashed together to form a sort of raft, a 'log boom' they say, which is steered by 'drovers' who ride on top in order to free up any log jams. It's a dangerous and skilled job, but luckily there are few accidents.

In that way they reach the saw mill first where they are sawn up and then taken to the pulp mill. There's a whole series of processes to transform the cut wood into wood-pulp. Instead of pulp mill everyone here just says mill because there are huge mill-stones inside to grind the wood down. Most of the wood-pulp is exported to Europe, so it's funny to think that you may be reading a newspaper in Gornac made of wood-pulp from Chicoutimi!

Forestry is as important here as vines and cereals are for us – I must get used to saying for you – and the town of Chicoutimi has grown because of the jobs created by logging. By the way, have I told you that Chicoutimi means 'where the deep water stops' in the local language of the Montagnais or Innu people?

Marie wants to write a few words now.

Bonjour Monsieur et Madame Duvigneau. Here life is different but not so different! Chicoutimi is a pretty town and at last the weather is warmer. I have made friends thanks to our cousins and have got to know the town well. I go to the general store for our food and stores. Compared with the Caïffa in Gornac the shop is enormous!

The store sells hardware and millinery. I really can buy anything there. But for wine it's not at all like Gornac. You have to go to a government run store. The State controls the sale of wine, beer and cider. And they are expensive.

Me again. Yes, Marie is right. Wine is expensive and frankly the beer is rubbish! People do make some wine at home unofficially, but it's nowhere as good as Gornac wine. They pick wild grapes like the first colonists. It's a bit like how the peasants used to make 'moon wine' in the Middle Ages at home.

There are vineyards in the area of course but I don't know yet whether I'll be able to work in one. The winemakers have to work fast between the first buds on the vines to the harvest because of the short summer season. Like at home the vines here don't like the cold, but here the cold is something else!

Jacques explained why there were so many floods when we arrived in May. It's a complicated story but briefly they built dams and created a huge lake to produce more electricity without any measures to protect the villages and the lands around the lake. The level of the water rose and farmers lost their fields and several villages had to be abandoned.

Well, that's all. We're going to bed now. I have to get up early to go to the mill. We look forward to your letters and news of home.

Lots of love from both of us

Alain and Marie.

Bernard handed the letter to Simone who began to read it again.

"Interesting. I had never heard of a pulp-mill before they went there," remarked Jacques. "One of these days I'd like to go and see these log booms myself. Just for a visit, I couldn't stand the cold for long."

Simone stopped reading the letter and looked anxiously at him.

"You must promise me, Jacques, you will never go to Canada. Losing one son is enough, two would be a tragedy."

"*Maman*, Alain and Marie are not lost as you put it. They are living there for the time being and will come back in a few years. Alain loves this area too much to stay in Québec for good. He likes his wine too much! To think the government controls everything, that's scandalous!"

"Perhaps, Jacques. But if that was the case here there would be fewer drunkards and fewer battered wives …"

"That's enough!" said Bernard getting up. "Let's eat. I'm hungry."

Chapter 22

Wednesday, 10th October 928

It was nine o'clock in the evening when Bernard entered the room he used as an office and sat down heavily in his chair. He was tired after a long day working at the vineyard. He picked up the bottle of Calvados and poured himself a small measure. He took a sip and pulled out some writing paper and his pen from the drawer. He hesitated for a moment before beginning to write.

Gornac, Wednesday 10th October 1928

Cher Alain, chère Marie,

Thank you for your second letter which has reassured us about your situation and your health, but which only arrived a couple of days ago. So, you will be in the middle of winter by the time you receive this reply. Do tell us more about the Tremblay family and give them my thanks for all they have done for you since your arrival.

Both your mother and I are well. You probably guessed, Alain, that after we received your first letter your mother organised an evening for all the family and invited the Marceau family and Paul Lasserre, Monsieur Coiffard from Espère, the mayor and the neighbours. The whole of high society Gornac! She made me read out the letter in front of everyone. You can imagine the discussion which went on after I had finished!

It seems we are not the only ones to have family who left for La Nouvelle France. If we are to believe all the fantastical stories of the exploits of our guests' ancestors we would have to believe they all set off with Champlain himself! It's even possible there are descendants of emigrants from Gornac in Chicoutimi! Everyone seemed convinced of it!

We were very busy in September as usual. The harvesting went well because it was warm and dry the whole month. We began on the 10th and it was all in by the 30th. We missed the two of you but we managed perfectly well without you nevertheless! The journeymen asked after you and they all send their best wishes.

The windmills in Gonin are starting to fall into ruin. It's sad to see. Some of the sails were brought down during a storm in August. The mayor says we must finish the job and bring down the remaining sails to make the windmills safe. The harvest festival still took place in Gonin as usual but further away from the mill towers. Everyone knew that a whole way of life had come to an end when they saw the terrible state the windmills are in.

Your mother wants to add a few words now.

My dear children, I'm so happy to know you are both in good health. The house you have described sounds wonderful, but I'm worried it will be difficult to heat during the terrible winter ahead of you. I just can't imagine such deep snow everywhere and the unbelievably low temperatures. You must buy really warm clothes and never leave the house. Have you got enough wood to keep you warm? And enough oil for the lamps? And electricity for cooking?

So you can see your mother never stops worrying about you. But I can't understand how she has forgotten to tell you that your sister Simonette had a little boy at the end of July – Alain-Marie, in your honour. Another mouth to feed.

Well that's all for the moment.

My best to both of you

Papa

Chapter 23

Thursday, 29th November 1928

As soon as Lucette Marceau learnt that Eugénie was pregnant, she had a telephone installed in the house. Now she was waiting anxiously for news from Francis. Eugénie had had complications during her pregnancy and Dr Lasserre had insisted she spend the last two weeks before the birth in hospital in Bordeaux.

Outside it was cold and a fine layer of snow and hoar frost had turned the roads and fields a sparkling white. Everyone was expecting a hard winter.

That autumn the brambles in the hedgerows were overladen with blackberries; the oaks had produced large acorns; the husks of the maize cobs were thicker than usual; the migrations south of ducks, cranes and swallows had happened earlier than normal. And to confirm these signs of a harsh winter to come, which all country people recognise, Lucette had discovered spiders all over the house.

She didn't put much credence on these old wives' tales herself, but even the forecasters on the wireless were starting to predict an unusually hard winter. She got up to put another log on the fire and turned the set on, more to provide some sound about the house than to listen to it.

She sat down by the hearth and thought over the events of the past year. She had been invited twice to the Duvigneau home to listen to Bernard read out the letters from Alain and Marie. She was relieved to know they were in good health and still enthusiastic about Chicoutimi. It was already six months since they had left and the villagers' memories of them were already beginning to fade, busy as they were with their own lives. Despite the rapid grape harvest, the good wheat and maize harvests, and the huge crop of fruit, people were starting to worry. There was talk of recession and in the towns workers were being laid off. The numbers unemployed were rising. The coming year of 1929 did not look as if it was going to be a happy one.

Lucette herself felt more alone than before. Léonce continued to be obsessed with the family jewels. He came to Gonin from time to time to search the house, but hardly ever came to see his sister. Each time she walked into the main village, she passed by the deserted house where Marie and her father had lived. The windmill towers with their broken arms watched her as walked between them, their blank windows like unseeing eyes.

Saddened by these thoughts, she was drowsing by the fire when the telephone rang.

"*Maman*, it's me. Everything's fine. We have a little daughter. Eugénie and the baby are fine. They have to stay in hospital for a few more days but they're both well."

"Congratulations, Francis. A little girl. That's wonderful. Give Eugénie and the little one a big kiss from me. Have you thought of a name?"

"We want to call her Odette, if you are agreed."

There was a moment of silence on the line.

"Hello, hello. Can you still hear me, *maman*?"

"Yes, of course. Odette, that's lovely. Your grandmother would have been pleased."

"Thank you, *maman*. I understand. Big hugs. I'm coming back to Gonin tomorrow because I have work there in the morning and I'll come and see you. We'll celebrate together."

"Thank you, Francis. Till tomorrow."

Too emotional to say more Lucette put the receiver down.

A minute later the telephone rang again.

"Lucette? It's Paul."

"Hello, Paul. Have you heard the wonderful news? Francis and Eugénie have a little girl."

"Yes, yes. That's why I'm ringing you. To congratulate you on being a grandmother. I'm very happy for you."

"Thank you. I'm delighted. They're going to call her Odette, like our mother."

"That's lovely. You must be pleased. I have more good news for you. Bernard has just received another letter from Alain and Marie. She's expecting a baby too in February. Simone is going to organise an evening as usual to read the letter to friends and family."

"That's marvellous. It's as if I have two grandchildren at the same time. I'm so fond of Marie, as you know."

"Good. I'll see you soon. I have to go. I have some home visits to make."

"Thank you for telephoning, Paul."

Chapter 24

Saturday, 1ˢᵗ December 1928

After the success of the evening when the first letter had arrived from Chicoutimi, Simone had decided to organise one each time there was a new letter. At the evening for the third letter the guests arrived at seven and went into the main room where a fire blazed in the hearth. While Bernard served drinks to the adults, the grandchildren tucked into bread and chocolate in the kitchen as tradition dictated at Grandma and Granddad's house.

Bernard proposed a toast to the 'emigrants' and took out the letter to read to everyone.

Chicoutimi, Thursday 8ᵗʰ Novemeber 1928

Chère maman, cher papa,

Thank you for your letter in October which we enjoyed greatly. I know that you were joking papa, but there are families here with names you all will recognise like Laporte, Langlois, Drouin, Garnier and Boucher. However, no-one has ever heard of Gornac!

As in France there are veterans of the Grande Guerre here. They are called the 'Vingt-deux' from the name of the Québecois regiment. The 'anglos' here pronounce it 'Van Dooz'! It's incredible to think people from here crossed the Atlantic to go to fight in France for us. They returned in 1919, but couldn't drink to their own return as there was prohibition! Luckily it did not last long in Canada unlike in the United States. The Québecois government simply took over control of alcohol sales itself! A neighbour who is a veteran told us that. He went to France in 1917 and fought at Vimy and Arras.

Great news about the grape harvest papa. You did finish quickly. Here winter has started and we have lots of snow. It was minus 10 last night, or 10 below as they here. Really hard to start the char, that is the motorcar, in the mornings. You can see we are starting to use Québecois words already! And yes, we have been able to afford to buy a small motorcar.

What you described about the windmills is really sad. Marie is very upset.

Work at the pulp mill has slowed down because the rivers are frozen and we are working just with the wood we stocked up with during the summer. To tell the truth the work has also slowed up because of the drop in demand from Europe for wood pulp. People are talking of a recession starting and Jacques is worried for the mill. He thinks we will have to lay off workers.

In winter we can't use the rivers so we go and work on sites around Lake Kénogami to fell timber for next year. The logs, or trunks, will stay here till spring. We pile them on the frozen river ice and simply wait for it to melt! Easy! As you can see I am learning a whole new trade.

But I've kept the best news till last. Marie is expecting our first child in February. She is well, tired of course, but that's all. Her cousins are looking after her and already we have piles of warm baby clothes people have given us and a cot and all the rest of the clobber!

I can already hear from here maman organising another grand evening to celebrate the news!

We shall miss you all at Christmas, but we will be surrounded by family here and there will be plenty of snow for the reindeer and Father Christmas's sledge.

We send you lots of love and wish you a happy Christmas and prosperous New Year.

Alain and Marie.

After Bernard had finished reading the letter, everyone began talking at once.

"That's wonderful news for Marie. A baby so soon! They didn't wait long."
"There probably wasn't much else to do on the ship during the crossing …"
"Bernard! Don't be lewd."

"It's strange to find family names there which are so familiar. I know people called Laporte and Garnier in villages around here."
"It's logical all the same. They are French people who emigrated. They're not going to change their names when they arrive!"

"It's so cold there. I couldn't cope with that. It's cold enough here and their winter is long, isn't it?"
"It was minus three one time when I was in Paris, that's a enough for me."
"Did he really mean it about the reindeer? Do they have reindeer?"

"During the war I was at Arras. I did hear of the 22nd Royal Regiment of French Canadians but I never saw any of them."

"Prohibition! That could never happen in France."
"But it would be a good idea ..."
"Simone! Don't start that again."
"It's just what I think."
"It's a good thing you aren't President of the Republic then."
"One day French women will have the vote and they will elect a woman as President, you'll see ..."
"Never in my lifetime!"

"We could send them a parcel of baby clothes and toys, couldn't we, Simone?"
"I'm afraid it would cost more to send than the clothes are worth."

The evening finished late and the parents had to carry their sleeping children back home.

Chapter 25

Saturday, 15th December 1928

Francis and Eugénie arrived early for lunch to Lucette's delight. She loved these family meals together. It was cold outside and she had lit a fire in the hearth. Odette was sleeping in her cradle. Eugénie helped Lucette lay the table while Francis went to fetch the apéritif. The three adults sat down by the fire.

They were discussing the latest news from the village when there was knock on the door. Lucette went to open it thinking it might be Paul Lasserre come to share the meal with them. But it was the postman. He held out a letter.

"There's a letter from Canada for you, Madame Marceau. I hope the news is good and wish you *bon appétit*."

"Thank you, Pierre. Come in out of the cold and have an apéritif with us."

"That's kind of you, Madame Marceau, but I must finish my round," he said, not wishing to delay the opening of the letter, which he knew she had been anxiously waiting for. "You can give me the news of the youngsters tomorrow."

Paul arrived at that moment and Lucette invited him in.

"Come in, Paul. You've arrived at the right moment. I've just received a letter from Québec. Come and sit by the fire, you must be cold."

She tore open the envelope forgetting to serve the apéritif.

"It's from Marie herself!"

She cleared her throat and read aloud, while Francis served the drinks.

Chicoutimi, Saturday 12th November 1928

Chère Madame Lucette,

You probably already know I am pregnant if our letter of the 8th arrived before this one. But I wanted to write to you myself to tell you the good news.

I am very well. Pierrette, Therese, Marguerite and Anne are all looking after me. They have explained everything about the doctors and the hospital.

We are both delighted. Starting a family shows our cousins and our new friends we really do mean to settle here and become Québecois.

Life here is pleasant. I have had to get used to living in a town with so many people. Chicoutimi is much bigger than Sauveterre, maybe three or four times the population, and there are shops where you can buy everything.

The general store is enormous as I wrote before. The first time I went I was afraid, as it looked so much like a grand hotel where only rich people could enter. But Anne, who was with me, just laughed and pushed me inside. I stopped in the doorway completely amazed. It was like Ali Baba's cave from A Thousand and One Nights. Even the shops in Bordeaux are nothing like it.

Everything you want to buy is stocked on shelves which go right up to the ceiling behind a long counter. We give our lists to the assistant and he goes to find everything. Often he has to go up a ladder to bring down items from the top shelves. We just sit on stools like ladies of leisure waiting for him to wrap up our parcels! It's great! I'm used to it now and the assistants recognise me when I go into the store.

A local product I have discovered and which I love is sirop d'érable. It's delicious! There's a lovely story about how the Indians discovered it thanks to the squirrels! They saw red squirrels licking the bark of maple trees. In fact they were not licking the bark but the juice oozing out, which they call the taffy or syrup. It's a bit like the way the resin comes out of the pines in the Landes at home but much nicer!

We are all set up in the house. This summer was quite hot and I went on walks – hikes – with my cousins in the mountains near to the town. It's pretty here. Often we would reach a high point from where we had a beautiful view over the fiords. They look like lakes, but in fact it's the river Saguenay. It's wide and blue when the sun is shining and it winds its way through the valleys between the mountains. It flows into the Saint-Laurent river. The sides of the valleys are rocky and often covered in trees which go right down to the water edge.

We saw ferries which link up the villages by following the coast and calling in to the local harbours. There are often no roads between the villages so the ferries are a life-line, not just bringing people but all sorts of goods too. We were so high up on the cliffs the boats looked like toys. Next year Alain has promised we'll go on a boat on the river with the little one.

There are fields of wheat and maize all around, but I haven't seen any vines yet. Alain has told you how the farmers around the lake lost their fields because of the flooding caused by the dams the government allowed to be built. I don't really understand much about it but I know that what happened was not fair and I'm sorry for the people who lost their homes and their livelihoods.

Alain likes the work at the pulp mill but he's afraid it will not last. In the newspapers there's talk of lay-offs. Unemployment in the town is growing.

We are beginning to get used to the snow and the cold. We have good warm clothes and the house is well heated. I don't go out much at this time of the year and am often on my own waiting for Alain to return. But I have made progress in patchwork which people here love doing.

We wives meet together in a group and we work on a bed quilt or even a sort of parka. Each one of us brings pieces of material, cloth or even leather. We make a selection to make quilts in a mix of colours. We all sow on the same quilt so it's truly a joint creation. Working in a group like this means I have made lots of friends.

I'm making clothes for our baby too. You would be proud of me, Madame Lucette, if you could see me.

It was 10 below yesterday evening, but my cousins told me it will get much colder soon. That makes me a bit afraid. The winter is long here. We will have to wait until May to have warmth. There is no real spring like in Gornac.

I hope you are well. Francis and Eugénie will have had their baby before you get my letter. Give them my love and congratulations, please. Say hello from me to Dr Lasserre – to Paul – when you see him.

Despite the problems I had, I miss Gornac and especially Gonin. I hope one day the mystery of the jewels will be solved and we will be able to return. I'm very sad to hear what has happened to the windmills. Papa spent his life working in his windmill, which he loved more than us my mother used to say! I don't like to think of it in ruins.

I send all my love to the three of you, in fact four now, and I'll always be so grateful for all you did for me.

Marie

When Lucette had finished reading all four of them had tears in their eyes. They could feel Marie's homesickness. To think they would not see her for a long time saddened them greatly.

"Well," said Paul, breaking the silence that had fallen between them. "She's in good health and expecting a baby, which is marvellous. That will change their lives for the better. And I promise you I'll find out the truth about the jewels."

"Thank you, Paul. Léonce in his way wants to solve the mystery of their whereabouts too, even if it means destroying the house!"

"Grandma, the two of us could do patchwork together like Marie. And with friends. People always need good quilts."

"That's a lovely idea, Eugénie," said Lucette, standing up. "We'll discuss it at table."

1929

Chapter 26

Saturday, 19th January 1929

They had risen early that morning and were having breakfast in the kitchen.

"Don't worry, my sweet. I'll be with Jacques and Étienne and their friends. They know the mountains like the backs of their hands."

"I know, Alain, but you've never hiked with those funny snow shoes before."

"I've been practising in the garden and in the street. It's not that difficult. The only problem for me will be to keep up with the others who are so used to them and probably fitter than me. But I feel fit now after all the work at the mill. It'll be fine."

"Marguerite is going to spend the week-end here with me. I don't want to be alone. The baby could come at any time."

"But you've still got a few weeks to go before the birth."

"Let's hope you're right, but babies are not like trains, they don't keep to a timetable!"

There was a knock on the door and Alain went to open it to Jacques and Marguerite.

"Welcome!"

"*Salut, Alain.* You ready?" asked Jacques.

"Yes, I think so. Where are we going exactly?"

"Since it's your first excursion I've planned something simple. There's an old portage trail which runs alongside the

Chicoutimi river and leads to the new dam called the Portage des Roches. It's about ten kilometres to the dam from where will join the path. We'll be back this evening, but quite late. Next time I've a longer hike in mind including a night in a cabin."

"Excellent! Good. Let's go," said Alain shouldering his pack and picking up his snow shoes.

He turned to Marguerite.

"Thanks for coming to spend the night here. Marie is worried the baby will arrive earlier than planned."

"She's right. It's always possible …"

"I know. Babies don't work to time-tables!"

The two men left the house to join the other hikers in the waiting cars.

"We're going by motorcar to the start of the trail," explained Jacques. "The engineers built a new road to the dam, but we'll take the traditional portage route."

"Portage of what?" asked Alain.

"Canoes. Trappers and indigenous people used the rivers like we use roads, but often there were stretches impassable by canoe, either because of waterfalls, rapids or simply because the river was not deep enough for a loaded canoe. So, they had to carry the canoe along the bank to get round the obstacle."

"Impressive! They were tough people. Canoes are heavy."

"Yes, but canoes in this part of the world are not carved out of solid tree trunks like the dugout canoes on the west coast. Here they are made of birch bark on a frame, so, much lighter. But you're right all the same, they were tough guys those fur trappers!"

They parked by the side of the road and left the relative warmth of the vehicles. The group prepared for the hike first strapping on their snow shoes, called *raquettes.* Étienne showed Alain how to attach them firmly to his boots with the leather thongs.

They pulled on parkas, hats and gloves and beaver fur hats. They carried a backpack each with food and water. To Alain they all looked like real fur trappers, just as he had imagined them from pictures in his school books in France.

"You'll see, Alain. Once we're walking you won't feel the cold. The effort will keep you warm. We're going to take this narrow path leading to the river and then pick up the old portage trail," said Étienne, shrugging on his backpack.

"You'll need poles in some paces where the trail climbs," said Jacques, handing him two canes with small discs on the end.

"Everyone ready? Let's go."

It took Alain a few minutes to get used to placing his feet wider apart than normal as he moved forward. At first he tripped himself up by placing the edge of one raquette on top of the other, but quickly learned how to avoid doing that and was able to walk as fast as the others. The snow shoes stopped him from sinking into the snow and made him appreciate the talent and skill of the native peoples who made them.

After a quarter of an hour they reached the river. There was a pause while everyone retightened the straps on the raquettes and adjusted their backpacks.

"Now we are going to follow the river. In places the trail is narrow and steep. Whatever you do don't rush. You don't want to slip. The water is cold and the ice near the bank is not thick enough to hold you! We will wait for you if you fall behind," Jacques reassured him, giving him a tap on the shoulder.

The group set off in single file. Alain soon got used to the pace the others set and even dared glance around him instead of constantly looking at where he was placing his feet. Everything was in black and white; there was not a trace of colour. In their thick covering of frozen snow, the trees looked like white sharp-pointed candles perched on black trunks like stalks.

In the rare places where the ice on the river parted the water showed as thin ribbons of impenetrable blackness flowing fast under sheets of ice which reminded him of the pack-ice in the Saint-Laurent river. The sky was cloudy and grey, the silence almost total, broken only by the noise made by the hikers' footsteps and the cracking of the ice on the water.

"Jacques? Will we see beaver lodges on the river?"

"No, not here. Partly because of the dam and because the Chicoutimi is shallow here. But another time we'll take you higher into the mountains where we will see their dams and lodges."

"Unfortunately," added Étienne, "beavers have been over-hunted for a century or more and have become quite rare. The trade in their furs was too profitable. The authorities are now talking of creating no hunting zones and imposing permits. There will always be *'coureurs des bois'* – poachers, – but it will make it more difficult for them to sell their furs."

The group continued along the river. They didn't talk much, needing all their energy to negotiate the narrow stretches and to climb the steep slopes which overlooked the river below.

Alain had to stop several times to give himself a break and to catch his breath. To his relief he was not the only one. On one occasion he noticed a bird which seemed to be following them.

"Have you noticed that tiny grey bird? It's as if he's following us," he said. "He's funny."

"It's a Whisky Jack. The Whisky Jacks stay here all through the winter. I don't know how they find enough to eat," replied Édouard, one of the friends. "I love them. They are brave little birds."

"Great name and they're pretty too!"

"You're right. You'll see. He'll follow us until we stop to eat."

After walking for three hours they could see the dam through the trees. They stopped and one of the friends scooped out a hollow in the hard ground. He took a handful of dry kindling from his backpack and soon he had created a blazing fire. Jacques made a hook out of a triangle of branches and hung a pot full of snow over the flames to make a beverage which Alain had difficulty in recognising as coffee, but he nonetheless appreciated the warmth of a hot drink.

"In spring and in summer you have to protect yourself here from insects which drive you mad. The Algonquins cover their faces with fat, but you can also rub the sap of plants like the bloodroot into your skin. That works."

"Never heard of it," said Alain. "I've so much to learn here."

*

Marie and Marguerite had spent the morning doing housework. They had set up everything ready for the arrival of the baby; the cot, lent by cousin Anne, the bowl they would use as a bath, the little clothes and the nappies.

"There. It's all ready. The baby can come now!" said Marguerite. "You've done enough this morning, Marie. I'm going to prepare dinner. You need to eat."

"Dinner? But it's only midday!"

"That's right, you say 'lunch' at midday. Odd! Afterwards we'll chat for a bit and then you must have a rest."

They went downstairs to the kitchen and Marie sat in the rocking-chair while her cousin busied herself preparing the meal.

"Marguerite, you don't think they'll be too cold on the hike, do you? It's so cold outside and there's so much snow. Alain is not used to it."

"Bof! This is nothing today. Don't worry. Walking with raquettes will keep them warm. And they'll make a fire when they stop for a collation."

"A what?"

"Something to eat. A snack," she said, laughing. "You've still a few local expressions to learn, my dear."

*

The men were warming themselves round the fire and each was munching on the collation of bread and cheese that their wives had prepared for them They teased Alain when he called it a snack and amused themselves imitating his Bordeaux accent.

"But seriously, Alain. You've done well with the raquettees. It's not always easy when we have to go up and down on the trail."

"Thanks, Jacques. I am impressed with them. For walking in the snow they're really good. Trappers and native people certainly knew how to adapt to the environment. In the Gironde snow is pretty rare. We're more likely to need stilts for walking in marshland!"

They put out the fire and got ready to continue the hike. Alain dusted off some breadcrumbs onto the ground and the Whisky Jack was down in a flash to eat the bounty.

"Now he'll follow us for hours," said Édouard.

"We're going to cross the dam and return on the other bank to get back to the cars," said Étienne. "Everyone ready? Let's go!"

They walked on to the new Portage des Roches dam. The wind was blowing hard and the temperature dropped fast in the wind chill off the water. They stopped for a brief moment to show Alain the Kénogami Lake and to point out in the distance the Île à Jean-Guy, but didn't delay, wanting to reach the relative shelter of the trees on the north bank of the river.

"It's on Lac Saint-Jean where they built the dams which caused the water level in the lake to rise and, in some people's opinion, they deliberately flooded the fields and villages. Some say that it was because the owners of the new aluminium factory needed to increase the production of electricity. But that's all politics," said Étienne.

"Portage des Roches is *Ashini Kushnapagan* in the language of the Montagnais, the original inhabitants of the region," said Jacques in order to change the subject. "It's like Québec, which means 'narrows' in their language.

Just like Detroit means 'narrows' in our language thought Alain.

When they reached the other side it was nearly four o'clock and it was beginning to grow darker and colder. They again picked up an old portage trail for the return trek. The Whisky Jack was still following them, as Étienne had said he would.

"Hunters have told me they've seen wolves recently in this area," said Étienne. "We must keep a watch out, but with our torches now it's dark under the trees we're in no danger."

"Is that why Édouard is carrying a rifle?"

"Yes, but don't worry, your Whisky Jack will alert us if there's any danger."

After three hours walking they reached the bridge at Laterrière-Bassin where they could cross the river. Soon they were back at the cars. Alain was exhausted and fell asleep on the way back.

Arriving at the house there were no lights on inside. A message was pinned to the front door:

'We're at the hospital. The baby is coming. Get here fast.'

Chapter 27

Thursday, 24th January 1929

Simone Duvigneau shivered. It was cold outside. On the wireless the weather forecasters were saying it would be the coldest winter of the century. The coldest since 1895. In Gornac a blanket of snow lay several centimetres thick on the fields. The vines each offered their single black branch up to the sky like so many dead arms. The veterans of the Grande Guerre said the vineyards reminded them of the graveyards on the battle fields.

Simone however didn't find the scene sad. It was a lovely morning and the snow sparkled in the sun almost blinding the onlooker. She thought it quite fairy-story-like. She could make out animal tracks in the snow: deer, hares or wild boar perhaps. But despite the beauty all around her, Simone was anxious.

She was on her way to see Lucette Marceau in Gonin. It was near the end of January and they had had no news from Chicoutimi since before Christmas. Was everything alright? How on earth could they survive temperatures of minus 30 or lower? Poor Marie. Pregnant and so far from her family and Lucette. Shouldn't we have kept her here in the bosom of the family and faced down the rumours which condemned her? she fretted. Too late now.

She walked on between the windmills on the hill: three great stone towers with no reason to exist any more. On her left Marie's former home was still empty and forlorn. She reached Lucette's house halfway down the hill and knocked. The door opened immediately.

"Welcome, Simone," said Lucette, kissing her on both cheeks.

The two women had become close since Alain and Marie's departure. Two mothers who had each lost a dear child with whom their only contact was the rare letters from afar which they waited impatiently for each morning, looking out for the arrival of the postman.

"You've come at the right moment. I've just received a letter from Marie!"

"Ouf! I'm so relieved. I was worried something was wrong. It takes such a long time for letters to arrive and she wrote the last one in November."

Simone was so overcome that she had to sit down immediately.

Lucette quickly fetched her a glass of water.

"Right, I'm going to make us both a coffee and then we will read the letter together. Just relax by the fire. Don't move. It won't take a minute."

Chicoutimi, Sunday 6th January 1929

Très chère Madame Lucette,

I miss you so much. Don't worry, I'm alright but this evening is the Fête des Rois and I remember the evening last year at your house and how you invited Alain to the meal knowing he was going to propose to me. I was the only one who didn't know! Just one year ago! My life has changed so much since. In four weeks I'll be a mother myself.

"That's right. Wait while I work it out. She wrote this about three weeks ago. So, it will be for next week!" said Simone.

"Perhaps Alain will telephone when the baby arrives."

"Let's hope so."

I'm getting used to the winter. It's often sunny but really cold. Today it was only 10 below, but it's very damp and the wind is cold coming from the Saint-Laurent or from the mountains in the north. So it feels like minus 15. I don't go out much as I'm afraid of falling. The streets and wooden sidewalks are very slippery. It's Alain who goes to buy the provisions, as they say here.

At Christmas we went to Uncle André and Aunt Louise's. (It's lovely she has the same name as my dear mother.) The family is very kind and everyone came. Twelve children! It was all very festive. Aunt Louise and Marguerite and Anne had prepared a marvellous meal of their traditional Christmas turkey cooked with savoury and with cranberry and brandy sauce, decorated with wild grapes. It was delicious I promise you!

"A turkey cooked with savoury and with sauce made from cranberries! Can that really taste good? You're sure they were French before, Simone?"

"Of course! They have to make do with what is available there, I suppose. Turkey at Christmas though! I prefer a good roast goose and *foie gras*, and oysters if possible."

"And what do they do for wine?"

"Wine made by the government certainly doesn't tempt me."

Alain is learning to cross-country ski and how to walk with the 'raquettes' that you strap onto your shoes here so you can walk in deep snow without sinking in too far. He's going to go on his first hike soon in the mountains with Jacques, Étienne and some friends. He'll tell you all about it when he writes to my parents-in-law.

I'm tired now and will stop.

I send you all my love, Madame Lucette, and to Francis and Eugénie and of course to the little one. I hope to meet her before she grows up too much. Do tell me her name when you write.

Your loving daughter

Marie

Lucette wiped away the tears running down her cheeks and said:

"It's true. She's like the daughter I never had. Albert would have loved to have had a little girl."

Simone put her arms around her and they said nothing for a moment.

"But what is all this about rackets, *raquettes,* attached to their shoes?" said Simone. "I don't understand. Does she mean tennis rackets? That would be funny to see. Don't they have any good boots?"

The two women burst out laughing.

Chapter 28

Wednesday, 20th February 1929

Chicoutimi, Friday 25th January 1929

Chère maman, cher papa,

Now we are maman and papa too! Parents! And you are mamie and papi yet one more time!

Mariette was born on the 20th January just after midnight. I had been on a hike with Jacques and some friends and we were amazed when we returned in the evening to find no lights on in the house and a message on the door to go to the hospital. The little one arrived a fortnight early.

Luckily, cousin Marguerite had spent the day with Marie and drove her to the hospital before we returned. We rushed there and received a good telling off from the girls as you can imagine. We waited of course for the baby to arrive despite being exhausted after the hike.

Mother and baby are fine. Mariette weighs two kilos 20g, maman – I know you will want to know her exact weight. They will stay in the hospital for a few more days. Marie is tired but very happy, like me of course. I must get the house ready for their return, but I haven't had much time thanks to invitations to drink to the health of the new Québecoise from friends and neighbours.

Right. I must tell you about the hike we did in the mountains, because later I won't have time to write to you at leisure. I do have the impression though that it will be the women in the family who are going to look after everything. The men are supposed to keep out of the way! Ouf!

The hike was well worth a telling off all the same. We set off early by motorcar to go to an old portage trail which runs alongside the river Chicoutimi. It's a bit like a haul road along a canal, but if you are travelling by canoe you often have to take it out of the water and carry it on your shoulders to go round rapids, rocks and so on. Luckily canoes in Québec are made of birch bark and fairly light.

We had to wear raquettes – snow shoes – which look like tennis rackets to be able to walk in the deep snow. They have a frame made of ash or pine. The 'sole' is like a net or latticework woven from thin strips of leather. They are much wider than your boots of course when strapped on, so it's not easy to walk to start with but you soon get used to it. They are very effective at stopping you sinking into the snow.

But I think all this will interest you papa more that maman who is already becoming bored! Mariette has blond hair, blue eyes, pretty little hands and sweet little toes. Everyone says she looks like Marie, but I think it's too early to tell. She's just a darling, that's all!

Right, that's it. I'll send photographs later. I must go to the hospital. Luckily it's not far because it's still snowing and the roads are icy.

We send you lots of love. Remember us to everyone.

Alain, Marie and Mariette. xx

*

Gornac, Wednesday 20th February 1929

Chère Marie, cher Alain,

We have just received your letter and are replying immediately. What a shame it takes so long for letters to arrive. Congratulations! What a joy to have a little girl. Everyone here is so pleased for you and send you their love and congratulations. The arrival of Mariette has been well celebrated here! We are all impatient to see photographs of the three of you.

You missed Alain-Marie's baptism at the end of November and of course Christmas with us. Perhaps next year you will be able to come back to see everyone.

Winter has been hard here. It's cold and we have had several centimetres of snow, especially in Gonin up on the hill but also at Espère in the valley. Your funny raquettes would have come in handy!

The mayor is not well. He is suffering from the cold like others in the village. Your nieces and nephews love playing in the snow as you can imagine, but they have all caught colds of course. We're longing for spring to come.

Lots of love from all of us. Write soon and tell us how Mariette is getting on and don't forget the photographs.

Kisses from the two of us. We miss you so much

Maman et papa

Chapter 29

Tuesday, 15th May 1929

Lucette took her responsibilities as grandmother very seriously. Little Odette spent most afternoons with her while Eugénie worked at the *mairie.* She had established a routine after lunch of pushing Odette in her perambulator through the vines which were coming into bud. After the past harsh winter she was pleased to feel the warmth finally return.

Her sister Élise's house had remained unoccupied since her death. To Lucette's annoyance, Léonce had resolutely refused to sell it. It wasn't so much that she had great need of her share of the inheritance, although it would have been useful, but rather because she didn't like to see the state of the house worsen and the value reduce.

She was passing by the house as usual on her walk and was surprised to see her brother's new motorcar parked outside the open front door. From inside she could hear the sound of hammer blows and splintering wood. She knocked on the door and shouted her brother's name, but there was no reply. She went inside leaving the perambulator outside.

She shouted his name again more loudly this time. Léonce replied as he came down the stairs.

"*Bonjour, Lucette,*" he said, kissing her on the cheeks.

"*Bonjour, Léonce.* What are you doing? Have you finally decided to sell the house? I heard banging. Are you making some repairs?"

"What do you think I'm doing, for fuck's sake? No, of course I haven't decided to sell the house and I'm absolutely not making any repairs, rather the opposite. We must find those bloody jewels first. If that bitch didn't steal them, they must be here somewhere."

"So you finally admit Marie isn't a thief. The poor girl couldn't stay in the village because of your accusations ... "

"Stop right there, Lucette. I made a mistake, that's all. She didn't need to leave if she was innocent."

"As usual, you don't understand anything. Well, she's gone to Canada to start a new life far from here. Perhaps in the end you did her a favour. But what are you doing upstairs? Are you tearing everything down?"

"I'm searching everywhere. It's my house. I'll do what I like."

"You're a notary for goodness sake! You know the house is mine too. And I want to sell."

"And hand the jewels to the new owner? You're stupid. First we must find them. Then we'll see."

"I simply don't believe any more there are any jewels. You're just imagining them."

"But what if I'm right? Don't you want your share?"

Outside Odette woke up and, finding herself alone, burst into tears.

"I must go," said Lucette, looking furiously at her brother. "Just don't destroy the house completely. One of these days we will sell it and I'm sure it's worth more than these famous jewels of your imagination."

She turned on her heel and went out to look after Odette. Léonce, after a moment's hesitation, went back upstairs hammer in hand.

*

Two weeks later Francis was walking past his aunt's house with Eugénie and Odette on their way to have Sunday lunch with Lucette when they heard sounds of someone working in the garden. Their uncle was busy digging over the soil.

They stopped to say hello.

"*Bonjour, mon oncle*. You're doing a good job. Are you making a vegetable patch?"

Léonce looked tired, with bags under his eyes. His clothes were threadbare and he seemed exhausted. He leant on the handle of his fork and looked at his nephew.

"A vegetable patch! What a genius idea! Plant some vegetables, you say. No, nephew, I'm not doing all this work just for the sheer pleasure of it. I'm sure my sister must have buried the jewels here, since they're not in the house."

"You're still searching for the jewels, uncle? You're making yourself ill for nothing. If you want money, sell the house and give my mother her share."

"How dare you speak to me like that. I won't sell the fucking house until I have found the jewels. I know they are here somewhere."

He turned away and went back to his manic digging taking no more notice of his nephew.

Francis left quickly with his wife and daughter.

"He's making himself ill," he said to Eugénie. "He ruined Marie's life and now he's ruining his own. I'm going to telephone my poor aunt Agnès to see how she is. How can she live with a man like that?"

Lucette was delighted to see them when they reached her house. She was in the kitchen preparing the meal and Eugénie went to help her. Odette was still asleep in her perambulator, so Francis pushed it outside into the garden.

When they were seated round the table Francis told his mother what happened when they saw Léonce.

"I know. He's so obsessed that he's neglecting his practice in Bordeaux. Agnès is at the end of her tether and can't take it any longer. She told me she's going to leave him and go to stay with her sister in Blaye. She thinks Léonce will hardly notice she's gone in his present state of mind."

"That's ridiculous! Why doesn't he sell the house if needs money?"

"It's not that. He doesn't need the money. He wants the jewels. And it's too late for the house. Have you seen the mess inside? He has destroyed everything: the furniture, the floors, the stairs. Everything. The house is uninhabitable."

"*Oh maman*! I'm so sorry. The house belongs to you too. He doesn't have the right to do that, it's your inheritance."

"Don't worry, Francis. I'm happy here, I have all I need, I have a granddaughter I adore, a marvellous daughter-in-law and a perfect son. That's worth more than all the money in the world."

Chapter 30

Thursday, 21st June 1929

Chicoutimi, Thursday 30th May 1929

Mes chers parents,

Finally spring has arrived. It was a hard winter with lots of snow. We had to pull on boots, parkas, gloves and our beaver fur hats (as if going on a hike!) every time we wanted to go to the store, shop!, to buy food. It was fifteen below for weeks. People here are used to spending months indoors. That's hard for us. Going out even for a moment without being well wrapped up is dangerous.

Of course we never took the little one outside. We had to keep her warm. But she is doing well and has grown a lot. She's five months old already and weighs over six kilos. The nurses are pleased and say she has made good progress. I hope you received the photographs we sent you.

These last few days we have at last been able to go out into the garden and let her sleep in her perambulator on the deck at the front of the house. Marie is well and like me is happy to have some warmth and to be able to go out more often.

At the mill during the winter the work slowed down but is back to normal now. The ice on the rivers is melting and the log booms are coming down-stream. To be honest the talk here is still of recession and Jacques and Étienne are concerned for the future. Uncle André is not saying much but he's worried the mill won't be able to continue for much longer. He looks tired. If the worst happens we'll have to find other work but there's not much going near here. The unemployment rate is rising.

There are thousands of unemployed here in eastern Canada. The government is encouraging people to leave the towns and is offering plots of land in what they call the Grand Nord. Creating a farm by clearing the forest for ploughing would be incredibly difficult. Those people will go through very hard times to create a life for themselves.

Next week to cheer us up we're going to take a boat trip with Mariette up the Saguenay fiord. It's really pretty when the sun is out. I also want to plant some vegetables in the garden soon as the season is short. Tradition here says there are 140 days between sowing and harvesting cereals, and for the grapes to ripen, before the cold returns. But this year it has remained cold until the end of May so we've lost a few weeks already.

It's late. Marie and the little one are asleep. Mariette will wake around five o'clock for her feed. I'll get up around six to arrive at the mill by seven. I hope the frosts are over in Gornac and that the vines are in full flower. I miss seeing spring in the vineyard.

Lots of love to everyone. We look forward to your letters which we love receiving.

Your loving son

Alain

*

Gornac, Thursday 21ˢᵗ June 1929

Chers enfants,

How lovely to receive the pretty photographs of Mariette and the two of you. She is a real sweety. I imagine she has grown a lot since your letter and will soon be ready to walk.

Alain, you were only ten months old when you first walked. You were always in a hurry to follow your brothers and it was difficult to hold you back when they went off to the vineyard. Jean-Luc was in much less of a hurry. He was a year old before he decided one day to stand up. I think he wanted to go out to play with Simonette. Marguerite and Jean-Bernard were thirteen months old before they took their first steps on the same day, hand in hand like good twins!

How I do go on! If I continue like this I'll tell you the dates of the first steps of all our grandchildren.

Send us more photographs of the little one and if possible photographs of the Tremblay family and their children and of your house and of the town. Papa would like a photograph of his uncle and aunt. I enclose a photograph of us all taken at Christmas.

There's not much news from Gornac. The mayor is better now the warm weather is here and he has bought himself a motorcar. There are several motorcars in the village now. They go too fast in the streets and I was almost run down the other day in the place du marché. The drivers don't keep to the speed limit.

The carter Albert Despagne is seriously thinking of encouraging his son to train as a motorcar mechanic! They are receiving fewer and fewer orders for wooden carts now. I think that one day they will have to abandon cart making and set up what they call a garage for repairing all these motorcars.

Paul Lasserre is still practising in the village, but I know he wants to find a position in Bordeaux to be closer to his fiancée. We'll be sorry to see him go.

There, I must stop and prepare supper as Jeanne is on leave today and your father will be back soon from the vineyard.

Love and kisses to all three of you

Maman

Chapter 31

Sunday, 25th November 1929

Chicoutimi, Tuesday 5th November 1929

Chère maman, cher papa,

You must have heard over there about the stock market crash a week or so ago in the United States. The effects are already being felt here and the number of lay-offs is brutal. There is no unemployment benefit and people are suffering. In the towns volunteers have already set up soup-kitchens where they hand out bread and hot meals to people who have lost their jobs. The situation is serious.

For the moment the mill is still running, but Uncle André has decided to stop producing newspaper wood pulp in the New Year. That means we won't go to cut timber by the lake this winter. We'll go on making pulp until the present stock of timber runs out and then Uncle André will close the mill. For him it will be retirement, for us – we'll have to wait and see.

In the papers it says the recession is affecting Europe and France too. I hope the effects in Gornac are less and you are not suffering too much. People always want wine after all!

Enough pessimism! Mariette and Marie are very well. Marie worries of course, but I am sure I'll find something. Jacques and Étienne have lots of contacts in the area and we will find jobs.

I attach some photographs of Marie and Mariette and of the Tremblay family. I hope they will arrive before Christmas. We wish you all a Happy Christmas and a prosperous New Year despite everything.

Your loving son

Alain

*

Gornac, Sunday 1st December 1929

Mon cher fils,

Thank you for the lovely photographs of you and the family. I recognise my uncle André and aunt Louise but not the others of course. The photographs of Mariette and Marie are sweet. I have the impression from the photograph of you that you have put on some muscle. All that work in the forests and at the mill has toughened you up!

Your news about the mill and what is happening in Québec saddens and worries me. You know you can always return to France if life gets too difficult over there. We would be delighted to see all three of you back in Gornac. I don't like to think you won't have any work and not enough income to live comfortably.

In France the recession is seen mostly as an Anglo-Saxon affair. Here the consequences of the crash are less severe. Unemployment has risen, but on the whole all is well, especially in the countryside where there is plenty of work on *the land and we are continuing as before. As you say people still want their wine!*

The harvest this year went well. The journeymen worked hard and we brought everything in safely despite two short storms at the end of September. We are going to bottle the white next week. The quality is good after a sunny summer and the sugar content is excellent.

The family is all well and everyone sends you their best wishes for Christmas and the New Year. I wish you the best of luck at the mill and hope you find another job. Perhaps vineyard owners will need workers to tend the vines in the spring. That's a job you know well after all.

When your letter arrived your mother was not at home. I told her you had sent the photographs, but that you had forgotten to include a letter in the envelope. I don't want her worrying about what is happening to you over there.

Don't forget you can return home whenever you want.

Your loving

Papa

1930

Chapter 32

Friday, 28th February 1930

André Tremblay closed the doors of the mill, turned the key in the lock and walked away. He turned round after a moment to look back at the building whose dark windows met his gaze with blank stares. He could feel the mill's resentment at what he had done.

Inside, the stock of cut logs was exhausted. The mill stones no longer turned. There was not a sound in the building. Even the river alongside was silent. André knew he would never again step inside this building where he had spent most of his working life.

It made him think of how Marie had described her father's reaction when he finally stopped work in his windmill in France.

He paused on the bank of the Chicoutimi to look up the river which was clogged with logs and branches caught in the ice. All was quiet too at the sawmill not far upstream.

He worried for his sons and for Alain and for their families. The situation in the town was not good. There was no work available, especially in winter. They would have to wait for spring to find a job. He would do his best to help them by asking around all his contacts, but he knew his friends were in the same bind as he was. What a catastrophe!

There were rumours of deportations of immigrants. Because of the disastrous employment situation and higher social costs involved, the government had decided on a policy of exclusion and expulsion. André promised himself he would do all he could to protect Alain and Marie and their little daughter from deportation.

Turning away from the mill he returned home without another backward glance to start his new life of retirement.

*

Sitting around the table in their dining-room Marie and Alain stared at each other in silence. They had no appetite and their evening meal was going cold on their plates. The final closure of the mill had not come as a surprise, but the shock of the actual moment had stunned them.

Alain poured himself some wine.

"That's it for Uncle André. He has spent most of his working life at the mill. Now he has the right to his retirement. He didn't want us to be there when he closed the doors for the final time. He told me he understood what your father had gone through when he shut down his windmill. But Uncle André has all his family around him and he'll enjoy his retirement."

"That's true. *Papa* was lonely at the end."

"We'll manage easily until the spring. We've enough savings and we can live simply. We won't be short of anything, especially of wood to heat the house. Jacques and Étienne told me they would be contacting their friends and everyone they know to find us work. We must just be patient, but we will find something."

"But there are so many people out of work, Alain. In the town I have heard wives talking amongst themselves about their husbands. All of them laid off. People have no money to buy food. In the paper it says a third of workers in Montreal have lost their jobs. They are even talking of expulsions of immigrants back to their countries of origin. Do you think we'll have to return to Gornac? Honestly, I wouldn't mind if the present situation continues."

"Not yet, but perhaps one day we will."

Marie left the table to give Mariette her feed.

Alain remained seated, sipping his wine, lost in thought.

Chapter 33

Wednesday, 23rd April 1930

In Gornac the village had just celebrated Easter and the Duvigneau family had joined other families to take part in the traditional ceremony marking the end of the transhumance. The shepherds from the Vallee d'Aspe in the Pyrénées and those from the Landes on their high stilts were preparing to depart with their flocks of sheep. They had come to spend the winter in the Gironde where their sheep could graze the grass between the rows of vines. As every year they had been welcomed by the owners of the vineyards who were pleased to see their soil enriched by the sheep droppings. Soon shepherds and sheep would leave together by train from the stations at St Brice, Caudrot or La Sauve Majeur.

The Duvigneau family was returning home after the ceremony when the postman called to them from his van.

"There's a letter from Québec for you which I think you have been waiting for for some time," he said.

"That's right. Alain sent us photographs before Christmas but we have had nothing since. I was very worried. Thank you, Pierre," said Simone, turning to the others. "Come on, hurry up everyone! I can't wait to open it."

Back in the house she opened the envelope and following the family tradition the whole family listened as Bernard read the letter out to them.

Chicoutimi, Thursday 3rd April 1930

Chers parents,

Finally some good news! I have found a job not far from Chicoutimi - in a vineyard!

"What does he mean, Bernard? He's working for André at the pulp mill, isn't he?" exclaimed Simone. "Has he been fired? What has he done?"

"Calm yourself, Simone," replied her husband, looking uncomfortable. "I'll explain."

"Explain what?"

"Listen."

He turned to include the others.

"Just before Christmas we received the photographs Alain sent us. I told you there was no letter with them. That was not true."

"Bernard!"

"Just listen! He told me the mill was going to close because of the recession in Canada and the United States. There was much unemployment and many people had lost their jobs. The situation was serious. The government was even talking about deporting recent immigrants ..."

" ... so they could have come back ..."

" ... perhaps, but Alain told me that he wanted to stay to help the family until the actual closure of the mill. I didn't want to worry you, so I said nothing about the letter."

The family reacted with angry incomprehension to his words, but Bernard put an end to the growing protests by saying firmly:

"May I continue to read the letter?"

Yes, in a vineyard! Uncle André knows the owner and he promised us – Jacques, Étienne and me – work the whole of summer until the end of the grape harvest and the gathering of the apple crop. The farm has an enormous apple orchard as well as the vineyard.

It's marvellous and we're lucky. Offers of work are rare. And it's my turn to show the cousins how to become vignerons like they showed me how to become a woodsman!

We are very relieved. The mill closed its doors at the end of February and since then we have all had to tighten our belts. Luckily Marie and I had saved some money and we managed. But it's sad and hard to see all those who have no job and who have to resort to the soup-kitchens to have enough to eat.

We are starting work at the vineyard after Easter. It's in a village with a pretty name – Sainte-Famille-de-l'île-d'Orleans! It's a few kilometres away and so we will have to set off early. But we can all go together by motorcar.

So, no need for you to worry any more. All is well.

Marie and Mariette are in good health. The little one has been walking since Christmas and plays with her cousins. She has started to talk – with the local accent she has picked up from her cousins! Us too. If we want to be understood we have to adopt their accent and expressions!

That's it for now. I wish you a happy Easter and a good summer. I'll tell you about the work in the vineyard and orchards in a few weeks.

Lots of love to everyone

Alain, Marie and Mariette.

"So you see, all is well," said Bernard, handing the letter to his wife.

He poured himself a glass of wine and prepared himself to face the reactions of the family who were still shocked that he had hidden Alain's letter from them before Christmas.

Chapter 34

Thursday, 20th November 1930

Lucette left the house to go to the village to do her shopping. It was a mild day and she was going to buy food at the market for the weekend. Francis, Eugénie and Odette were coming for Sunday lunch as usual and she wanted to cook something special as it was the little one's second birthday.

She walked between the windmills and as always Antoine Bourdet's abandoned mill made her think of Marie and Alain. She wondered how they were going to manage again this winter.

Bernard had confided in her about what was happening there when he received Alain's letter before Christmas the previous year with the photographs. He had needed to talk to someone, but he made her promise not to say anything to Simone.

After the April letter everyone was relieved, but it was already autumn now and the work at the vineyard must have come to an end. How were they going to survive a second winter in Québec without work?

In the village the postman called to her.

"There's a letter for you, Madame Marceau."

She finished her shopping quickly and hurried back home. Sitting by the fire she opened the envelope.

Chicoutimi, Saturday 1st November 1930

Très chère Madame Lucette

Forgive me for writing to you to pour out my heart, but you are the only person I can confide in without holding back: I am afraid.

Alain found a good job in a vineyard in the spring as you know. He and his cousins worked there the whole summer. Since Alain knows so much about grapes ad wine making he was asked to help in the winery after the harvest was in. But now the work is over and they must wait for next spring to go back there.

We have savings and I think we will survive the winter but it won't be easy. There are people here who can't pay their rent and have had to leave their homes. Because of this terrible recession the unemployment rate is horrendous and people are living on hand-outs and going to soup-kitchens. We are going to offer our third bedroom to a couple who have no roof over their heads.

Honestly, I am afraid of the winter and of what it has in store for us. I'd like to return to France, to Gornac. We have discussed it between us, but Alain wants to try to hold out for another year. He thinks next year he could become maître de chai at the vineyard, for the cider not for the wine! The farm has an enormous apple orchard, he told me.

There you are. I've said enough. Don't worry too much, we will survive. Alain has done everything he can to ensure we will be all right.

Wish Odette a happy birthday for me. I dream that one day she will play together with Mariette in your garden in Gonin.

I wish you a happy Christmas and a good New Year. You are always in my prayers.

All my love

Marie

"And you are constantly in my prayers too, my dear daughter," Lucette said out loud. "I must talk to Françis about sending them some money."

1931

Chapter 35

Monday, 11th May 1931

The motorcar arrived at six.. It was Jacques' turn to drive. He sounded the horn and Alain came quickly out of the house. He got in to the front seat beside Jacques. Étienne and their friend Édouard were on the back seat.

"Hi everyone," he said. "So, the year has come round and we have work again! The boss wants us to work for him for the whole season. We're lucky. He must have been impressed by the work we did last year."

"That's thanks to you, Alain. You taught us the skills," said Jacques.

"Fair's fair. You taught me what to do at the mill."

"The unemployment situation has gotten worse over the winter. In Québec the official rate is 20% this year."

"Lots of people have lost their homes as they couldn't pay the rent," said Étienne.

"That's true. The couple staying with us were kicked out of their house. Luckily they did find work in the end and the rent they pay us has helped us to survive the winter," said Alain.

"It's the same for us," said Étienne. "It's good to be able to help people like that."

"It's all so stupid. The stock market crash is a catastrophe for the man in the street, but the big bosses don't suffer at all. It's terrible ordinary working people are forced to rely on soup-kitchens when it was not their fault," said Édouard.

"The authorities are doing their best. The infrastructure projects they're organising are great, but they're only paying

35 cents an hour. No-one can live on that, as we well know!"
said Alain.

There was nothing more to be said and they fell silent until
they arrived at the vineyard.

Chapter 36

Saturday, 29th November 1931

Lucette was at home when Paul knocked on the door. She opened it and he entered holding a letter in his hand.

"*Bonjour, Lucette,*" he said. "I met the postman on my way here and he gave me this letter for you. It's from Marie."

"Thank you, Paul. Come in, come in. We'll read it together. Coffee?"

"I'd love one, thank you," he said, taking his coat off. "It's cold out there."

While she was making the coffee, Lucette asked:

"Tell me about Jacinthe, Paul, if you don't mind my asking."

"Not at all. Yes, it's all good. She's hoping to be transferred to Bordeaux in a few months time. I'm looking for a post in Bordeaux myself, and then bingo!"

Lucette laughed out loud.

"And then bingo, as you say! I'm so pleased for the two of you, but we're going to miss you when you leave the village, Paul. *I'm* going to miss you."

"Thank you, Lucette. I'm thinking of keeping my house and so we will often be back. I've made good friends here and love the village."

"Did you tell Jacinthe about Marie and the jewels?"

"No. I feel it's like a professional confidence. I know it's silly when the whole village is aware, but … if Marie returns one day with her innocence proven as I'm sure she will, it wouldn't be fair to her to know that even people from outside the village know of the affair."

"That's kind of you, but ..."

"I know, she's my fiancée. You're right. When I have found out the truth, I'll tell her all about it of course."

"Coffee's ready. Let's read Marie's letter."

Chicoutimi, Monday 10th November 1931

Très chère Madame Lucette,

It's already nine months since I last wrote to you. With a baby life is very busy as you know. All went well this summer. You already know Alain and the cousins were hired again at the vineyard. Alain's skills helped everyone and the owner was pleased to be able to hire such good workers.

The situation caused by the recession has hardly improved. There is still more and more unemployment. We were able to help a couple here at home by letting them have our spare room for a modest rent. With that and the money you so generously sent - huge thanks to you and Francis and Eugénie – and our savings, we got through the winter without any serious difficulties. But the whole situation will repeat itself because the work at the vineyard is over. Alain and his cousins have been laid off like last year with, luckily, the promise they will be rehired in the spring.

Please don't send any more money, we will manage alright this winter.

So, our plan is to get through the winter, to work throughout next summer to earn the money to buy our tickets to return home! Yes, really. We are planning to return to Gornac next year. Mariette will become Gornacaise.

We will miss the family here who have been so kind to us and have helped us so much, but frankly we won't miss the cold and the recession. We didn't time our arrival well three years ago, but who could have foreseen the crash? It's just not fair.

Alain is going to write to his parents to explain the situation to them. On the whole we are fine but we can't continue to live from hand to mouth year after year and we prefer to come home. I'll be really pleased to come back to France as you have guessed!

Lots of love and kisses. I am so happy to think we will soon be together again.

Your loving daughter

Marie

"She writes like a mature woman now. She's no longer a young girl," said Paul. "I'm so pleased they're coming back. We haven't suffered here much from the recession, but life over there is obviously not easy."

"No, it's a pity they arrived just before such a difficult time, but as she says who could have predicted such a thing?"

"Well, I must redouble my efforts to find out the truth of what happened to the jewels before they return. You haven't had any more thoughts yourself which could help?"

"No, our mother was very weak towards the end of her life. I still think she hid the jewels somewhere and forgot where."

"Is Léonce still looking?"

"Yes. The house is a ruin now. He has torn down everything and demolished the inside. He has almost lost his mind looking, but he's convinced they are there somewhere in the house."

"Frankly, me too."

*

At Domaine Le Frègne, Simone was reading the letter from Alain with increasing pleasure. Her dear son was going to come home with his wife and their daughter. All the family would be together once more. These last three and a half years since their departure for Canada had seemed an eternity to her. At last the end was in sight.

Bernard came into the living room and Simone handed him the letter. He sat down and said nothing until he had read to the end, but then looked up all smiles at his wife and said:

"We could send them the cost of the tickets so that they can come back earlier."

"No, Bernard, I want to see them as soon as possible like you, but we must let them work their plan. If not, they will come back with a feeling of having failed and chosen the easiest way out to leave Québec. No, they must leave heads held high after having done their best to succeed in such difficult circumstances. We must be patient and wait for them to carry out their plan."

"You're right, my dear. But I can't wait to see them."

"We'll celebrate this news at Christmas *en famille*. We wont tell anyone else yet, except Lucette and Paul of course, though they probably know already."

1932

Chapter 37

Monday, 13 May 1932

The atmosphere in the motorcar was heady. For each of the four men and their families the winter had again been hard. They had been well paid in the vineyard the year before and in comparison to others they had been lucky. But lasting a second winter with only the money earned during the five months work had not been easy. They all had children to feed.

They had even worked a few days in the autumn on the public works sites. That meant joining a queue early in the morning outside the site gates. Often, even in Chicoutimi, hundreds of men waited for a job to become free. Some even paid the foreman to keep their job for the next day. All four of them had soon abandoned this way of getting work and providing for their families.

Fortunately a company from British Colombia had made an offer for the pulp mill to Uncle André in January. The company had taken advantage of the disastrous state of the economy and he had had to accept a low price for the saw mill and the pulp mill. However he had been able to stipulate that the men of the family could maintain the buildings over the winter and that they should be paid properly. In that way he had looked after those families dearest to him. The company knew the maintenance would be done by those who knew the job best and so accepted the deal.

Now the four friends were looking forward to starting work again in the orchards and the vineyard. The weather was becoming warmer and they all preferred working outside in the sun. Working inside the buildings with no heating had been cold and exhausting.

Chapter 38

Friday, 10th June 1932

Heads turned at the arrival of the new motorcar in the village. Rumours ran rife. A Renault Plymouth Sedan 4 door is not cheap remarked knowledgeable and appreciative on-lookers when they saw the vehicle parked outside the village shop on the place du marché. "How did Marcel get the money to buy a motorcar like that?" they asked each other. "Certainly not from what he earns as a mason."

Marcel Vauvigne, master mason by trade, was very proud of his new acquisition and didn't give a damn what people thought. He was enjoying driving with all his family on board and had even motored all the way to Bordeaux with them. At last he was someone with status in the village.

Paul watched as Vauvigne drove by giving him a cheery wave.

"He's getting above himself, that man. I wonder how he can afford it. An inheritance perhaps?"

He continued on his way to Gonin reflecting on the mason's sudden unexpected good fortune.

*

Aristide Labruyère entered the house grumbling to himself. The young mason was in the terrible mood. He threw his bag of tools onto the floor and sat down heavily in his armchair by the open door of the kitchen which looked out onto the garden.

Georgette had seen him arrive and walk past her without a word while she worked on the vegetable patch. She abandoned her planting and followed him into the kitchen.

"So what's the matter with you? Don't I get a kiss? You look furious. What's happened?"

"Have you seen the new motorcar in the village?"

"Yes. Everyone's talking about it. I'm not interested."

"Do you know who it belongs to?"

"No. I told you. I'm not interested."

"Really? And if told you it belongs to Marcel?"

"Marcel Vauvigne? But how on earth can he afford to buy a motorcar?"

"Exactly what I was wondering."

"In fact I was chatting the other day with his wife and she was telling me how difficult it is for Marcel to find work and for her to make ends meet. They have four children to feed."

"But he's been working for weeks now for Beynard making Élise's house habitable again. Lucette has finally persuaded him to sell it."

"I thought he'd completely torn the interior apart."

"Exactly. That's why there's lots to do. But I can't imagine Beynard pays more than the minimum for the work."

"Aristide," Geogette reacted after a moment's thought, "you remember that business …"

Just at that moment Paul Lasserre came into the garden. He was feeling hot after walking too quickly in the heat of the afternoon.

"*Bonjour, docteur!* You look fatigued. Do come in. I'll get you some of my cold home-made lemonade."

"*Merci, Georgette,*" he said, wiping his brow and going into the relative cool of the kitchen with relief.

"*Bonjour, Aristide,*" he said, surprised to see the mason sitting in his chair at that time of the day. "Taking a break? I don't blame you. It's so hot today. But I'm pleased to find you here."

"*Bonjour, docteur.* To what do we owe the pleasure of your visit?"

"I wanted to talk to you about Marcel Vauvigne and his new motorcar."

"We were just discussing that," said Georgette. "I don't understand how he can afford it. His wife told me she can hardly make ends meet each week. She has four children to feed."

"And they are not in good health in my opinion. He's working at Beynard's, isn't he? Where Élise used to live?"

"Yes. But Beynard doesn't shell out his money easily," said Aristide. "When he offered me the job, I refused. I don't work for peanuts."

"Aristide, you didn't tell me!" exclaimed his wife. "You can't turn down work like that!"

"I can. You have to know how to choose. Better no work than be taken advantage of. I'm better paid at the château."

"So," interrupted Paul, "where did he get the money to buy a motorcar?"

"A moment ago I was reminding my husband of the business with the jewels and how poor Marie is now in Québec because of it. Have you had any news of her, by the way, doctor?"

"Not recently. You do know she has a little girl, don't you? She must be nearly four now."

"Yes, Lucette told me. I'm so pleased for her. She was a nice young girl. I never believed she had stolen the jewels. Beynard is a monster."

"Don't waste the doctor's time with those old stories," snapped Aristide.

"But what if the story is true?"

" ... that Marie did steal those bloody jewels?" responded Aristide in surprise.

"No, you dolt! That the jewels do exist and that even Élise didn't know where their mother had hidden them. Their mother never trusted the banks any more than I do, nor did Élise."

"What do you mean, Georgette? That the jewels were in the house despite Beynard's efforts to find them. You think Vauvigne might have found them while he was working inside?" asked Lasserre, intrigued.

"As I said he has been working for weeks renovating the interior, doctor," said Aristide. "Perhaps my wife is right …"

" … say that again!" said Georgette.

" … that he found the jewels or something else valuable while he was working."

"I'm sure you know, doctor, of the old tradition in the countryside: hide your valuables and money by the fireplace," Georgette said. "All you have to do is to remove a stone from the chimney-breast, scoop out a hole behind and replace the stone. Then you have a safe and dry hiding place."

"Marcel would have spotted the slight difference in the colour of the mortar when the stone was put back. Something an amateur like Beynard wouldn't have noticed," added Aristide.

"What do you think, doctor?" asked Georgette, pleased her husband agreed with her.

"And he might have sold the jewels in Bordeaux without telling Beynard what he had found? Is that it?" said Lasserre slowly thinking it through. "There's a way of finding out. Next time I'm in Bordeaux I'll make some enquiries."

He looked at them.

"But don't say anything to anyone in the meantime. It's a serious accusation. So be careful what you say."

Chapter 39

Thursday, 14th July 1932

It was a fortnight later before Paul had some free time to go to Bordeaux. He was impatient to see Jacinthe, but he hadn't forgotten his conversation with Georgette and Aristide. In the meantime he had made some enquiries by telephone round the pawn brokers to find out if they had received a quantity of jewellery recently, but had had no success.

He was meeting Jacinthe in their favourite restaurant, *Le Régent*, in the Place Gambetta not far from his studio flat in the Rue du Palais Gallien. She was living temporarily with her parents after being transferred from Biarritz to the hospital in Bordeaux. He had offered her his studio flat but she thought it would be more discreet to find her own apartment.

She was waiting for him at the table he had reserved and stood up to give him a kiss. He had brought her a bunch of red carnations and that earned him another kiss as she took them from him.

The waiter knew them well and immediately brought them two glasses of Loupiac. They spent a quarter of an hour catching up on the recent events in their lives before ordering.

"So tell me, what's happening in your tiny village in the middle of nowhere," said Jacinthe. "Are you still looking after old peasants who pay you with bottles of good wine?"

"That does happen from time to time ..."

"Or do you have a secret girl friend you don't tell me about? A young handsome doctor in a small village is bound to encourage fantasies in the minds of the local girls!"

"Don't mock, chérie. You can't imagine the amount of scheming and plotting that goes on in the countryside. Everyone knows everyone. If I had a secret girl friend on the sly someone wouldn't have failed to tell you, I'm certain."

"Well that's reassuring!"

"But seriously, I'll tell you later a true story about one of the young girls in the village. You'll perhaps be able to help me find out some information today. But first tell me more about your new posting at the hospital. Are the doctors there young and handsome too?"

The waiter arrived with their first course and the wine. The conversation changed direction while they were eating. Over coffee Jacinthe reminded him he was going to tell her a story about a girl in the village. Paul told her what had happened between Marie and Beynard and why the story had surfaced again.

"So that's the real reason Alain and Marie left for Québec! Why didn't you tell me before? No matter! That was so unfair on the young woman. But you think now the mason has found the jewels after all?"

"I think it's possible."

"So what do you intend to do?"

"I want to go round the auction houses in Bordeaux and find out if they have sold a quantity of jewels at auction in the last six months."

"You could telephone. That would be quicker."

"No, this time I want to question them in person. I telephoned all the pawn brokers with no luck, but I'm not convinced they told me everything. It's the nature of their business to be discreet. But if the jewels were really valuable, Vauvigne would have gone first to the auction houses if he had any sense. More chance of a better deal."

"You want me to come with you?"

"Yes, if you would. They'll agree to speak to me more easily if you are there, I'm sure."

"So you want to use me as the pretty lady who flirts with the *monsieur difficile* who claims client confidentiality and doesn't want to reveal the details of the sales? Is that it?"

"Who said you were pretty?"

"Touché! You win," she said, annoyed at having been so easily caught out. "But I'm doing it for Marie, not for you. And on condition you take me to your village again afterwards."

"Agreed!"

He signalled to the waiter.

"Deux coupes de champagne, s'il vous plaît."

Jacinthe looked at him in surprise, but before she could say a word he announced:

"I have some good news, chérie."

He made her wait while the waiter put two glasses of champagne in front of them.

"I applied for a post in Bordeaux as general practitioner and I have been accepted. So at last I can come permanently to Bordeaux."

"And disappoint all those young girls in Gornac!" she said, hugging him.

*

Paul entered Beynard's office building and asked for him at reception. He was made to wait half an hour before being received by the notary.

"He wants me to think he's overrun with work," thought Paul. "But everyone knows his practice is not doing well and that he has become somewhat of a loner."

Indeed when he entered Beynard's office he was struck by the tired and unkempt appearance of the notary. He had put on weight, his face was pale and puffy. He clearly was not taking care of himself.

'So it's true. His wife did go to her sister's,' he thought.

Beynard rose from his chair to greet him and to shake his hand.

"Bonjour, docteur. Welcome. How are you? It's years since we last saw each other. Are you still practising in Gornac? Please do take a seat."

He sat behind his desk and stared at Paul.

"Oui, maître," Paul said sitting in his turn in front of the desk. "But I'm going to move soon to Bordeaux. I've been appointed to a GP post here in the city."

"Good news for us, though not for the village. If I remember rightly you have a fiancée who is a nurse."

"You have a good memory! Yes, she's working now in Bordeaux too."

"So it's all turning out for the best. But I imagine you haven't come here to tell me that. How can I help you?" he asked, turning on his professional voice.

Paul took out a sheet of paper from his jacket pocket. He unfolded it and spread it out on the notary's desk. Beynard looked at it in surprise.

"What's this?" he asked, changing his tone and looking at Paul suspiciously.

"It's a list of jewels someone sold at auction three months ago."

"What's that got to do with me?"

"Look at the list carefully, maître. Do you recognise it?"

"No, I don't think so," he replied slowly.

"Doesn't it remind you of the jewels which belonged to your mother?"

"Perhaps," he replied, becoming more and more suspicious. "The last time I saw them I was very young. I wouldn't be able to tell you exactly what they were."

Paul took an envelope out his pocket and set before Beynard photographs of the jewels on the list.

He waited.

"Yes! Those are my jewels. Where the devil did you find them?"

"I didn't find them or sell them, Beynard. It was Vauvigne the mason who found them and who was stupid enough to use his own name when he sold them at auction."

"Vauvigne! The bastard! Where did he find them? I searched the house from top to bottom. It nearly drove me mad. So he stole them from me. I'll have him for that."

"Keep your temper, Beynard. If these are the jewels which belong to you and Lucette, that means they were somewhere in the house all the time. And that you falsely accused Marie Bourdet of being a thief."

"Well. Perhaps yes, but ... "

"There's no perhaps, Beynard. You forced her out of her village by accusing her without proof and you hastened the death of her father. You are a worm."

"How dare you speak to me like that, Lasserre?" he shouted standing up. "I ..."

He fell back into his chair and banged his fist on the desk in fury and frustration.

Paul stood and left the office without a word.

Chapter 40

Saturday morning, 16th July 1932

Bernard was working in the vineyard when Simone arrived and looked for him amongst the rows of vines.

"Bernard! Bernard! Where are you?"

Bernard straightened up, peered over the vines and shouted:

"Over here. What's the matter?"

"There's another letter. Come quickly."

He didn't need to ask who the letter was from and dropped the length of willow tie and the knife he was holding onto the ground before hurrying over to join Simone.

They went back to the winery together and sat on a bench outside the building in the sun. Simone opened the envelope and they read the letter together.

Chicoutimi, Friday 1st July 1932

Mes chers parents

Sorry not to have written sooner, but you are about to find out why we have been so busy.

Last winter was less difficult financially because we were working at the mill! No, it's not started up again. Uncle André sold it to a Vancouver company in January. He stipulated in the contract that the maintenance of the pulp-mill and sawmill should be done by us! So we spent the rest of the winter maintaining the machinery, the mill stones and the two buildings. Frankly it was sad to work in the silent buildings we love so much. It was cold and damp inside, but the work wasn't badly paid. So the winter was much less difficult than last year. Unfortunately, we all fell ill one after the other thanks to the damp inside and because the buildings are right by the iced-up river. There was no heating of course – the company wouldn't pay for that.

But now the warmth of summer has returned at last. We have all gone back to working in the vineyard in the sunshine. Our plan is still on track and we are counting on returning to Gornac in September.

Marie is suffering from a fever at the moment but the doctor says it's nothing serious and that the warm weather will do her good.

Alors, à bientôt, mes chers parents.

Grosses bises,

Alain

"How wonderful to know they will soon be with us," said Simone.

"André must have been sad to sell the mill. He worked there for forty years."

"True, but also pleased to rid himself of it under the present circumstances in Québec."

Just at that moment they saw Paul approaching.

"Good timing, Paul. There's a letter from Alain. They are definitely going to return in September."

"Excellent! And I have good news for you too."

He sat on the bench beside them and spent a few moments making himself comfortable.

"Paul! I know you too well, you're teasing us. Tell us!"

"OK. We've found the jewels."

He waited for them to calm down.

"Paul!" said Simone, shaking him. "Tell us everything."

"Vauvigne, the mason who was doing the repairs to Élise's house for Léonce and Lucette, discovered them beside the fireplace and he sold them at auction in Bordeaux."

"So that's how he got the money to buy the motorcar."

"How did you find them ?"

"I went round the auctioneers with Jacinthe. It was Georgette's idea that he had found the jewels, which would explain how he had been able to afford the Renault."

"And does Léonce know?"

"Yes, I went to see him in his office."

"And Lucette?"

"I've just come from seeing her."

"So, finally the mystery is solved and Marie's innocence is proven. Just in time for their return. Absolutely marvellous!"

"We should send them a telegram straight away to tell them the good news," said Simone.

"Excellent idea," said Bernard. "Paul, come to the house this evening to tell the family the whole story. I want to know every detail."

"And bring Lucette, and Francis and Eugénie. Paul, is Jacinthe with you?" asked Simone.

"Yes, she is."

"Bring her with you. We'd love to see her."

"Thank you. Till this evening then."

*

Chicoutimi, Saturday morning, 16th July 1932

Telegram received at 08.00 Saturday 16 July at the main post office in Chicoutimi, Québec, Canada, from Monsieur Bernard Duvigneau of Gornac, Gironde, France.

Delivered to Monsieur and Madame Alain Duvigneau, 7 rue Jacques-Cartier, Chicoutimi, Québec at 09.00.

JEWELS RECOVERED STOP VAUVIGNE ADMITTED EVERYTHING THANKS TO PAUL STOP WISHING MARIE GOOD RECOVERY STOP SAFE JOURNEY BACK SEPTEMBER STOP PAPA STOP

The postman knew Marie and Alain were away spending a few days in Québec City. Knowing a telegram is always important, he went to deliver it to André Tremblay.

"Thank you, Giles, you did the right thing. Marie is feeling better now and Alain wanted to cheer her up by visiting Québec."

The postman remained standing by the door and made no move to go.

André tore open the envelope and quickly read the message.

"This news will make her feel even better," he said. "Thank you again, Giles."

He closed the door leaving the postman standing there, his curiosity unsatisfied.

*

Gornac, Saturday evening, 16th July 1932

All the guests had left and in Bernard's office the two men were enjoying some quiet after all the excited reactions to the news that evening.

"Thank you, Paul," said Bernard. "You've proved my dear daughter-in-law is innocent. I have been told that Vauvigne has admitted everything. He'll have to sell his fine motorcar before he goes to prison. I'm sorry for his wife and children. It will be difficult for them."

"You must thank Aristide and Georgette for giving me the idea of checking round the auctioneers in Bordeaux."

"The telegram arrived in Chicoutimi, but Alain is away at the moment with Marie and the little one in Québec City for a few days. André will give them the good news when they are back if he can't reach them by telephone."

"They will be able to return here with their heads held high," said Paul. "But I'm certain Beynard will not apologize despite having got his jewels back."

"I'm sure you're right, Paul, but what does that matter now? Let's change the subject. I hear you're leaving us to go to Bordeaux?"

"That's right. I've been appointed to a GP position in the city. Now I can finally be near Jacinthe and we intend to marry soon. You and Simone will be honoured guests of course."

"Congratulations! Not before time! We must drink to that."

They went back into the living room where Simone and Jacinthe had finished clearing up after the guests.

"Simone, fetch some more glasses, would you? We must toast Paul's success in Bordeaux and this young couple's forthcoming marriage."

Chapter 41

Tuesday, 30th August 1932

Unusually Simone opened the letter from Alain without waiting for her husband. She was impatient to know their reaction to the telegram. Everyone had expected an immediate response to the good news, but the complete silence since had worried them. Simone opened the letter and began to read.

When Bernard came home at midday he found his wife slumped on the sofa in the living room being comforted by Simonette and Marguerite. All three women were in tears.
Simonette held out the letter to her father without a word.

Chicoutimi, Monday 16th August 1932

Mes chers parents,

This is not an easy letter for me to write. Marie passed away last week. She had been suffering from a virus for several weeks but the doctors did not think it serious and we all thought she would get better with the warmer weather. In fact she was feeling so much better that we decided to have a break and spend a few days in Québec with Mariette to show her the city.

When your telegram arrived at Uncle André's to say those cursed jewels had turned up at last, he tried to phone us but I had forgotten to give him the number of our hotel. It was I who telephoned him first to say that Marie had had a relapse and that she was in hospital in the city. He told me the good news and I went straight to the hospital sure that Marie would be delighted. When I got there she had sunk into a coma and I told her the news. I'm not sure she could hear me, though the doctors said it was possible.

I told the doctor about her being accused of stealing those jewels and he thought that subconsciously maybe she had never got over the accusation she was a thief and had lived with the feeling people still had doubts about her innocence. He said she was still very weak and perhaps the virus had made all those negative feelings come back to her. That plus the effort of coming to Québec had been too much and provoked the relapse. He was sure she would react well to the news when she came round.

She never came out of the coma and died two weeks later.

That's all I have the strength to write now. Mariette and I shall return on the Ausonia. We arrive at Cherbourg on the 15th September.

Bises,

Alain

Bernard sank heavily into his armchair just as the door opened and Paul entered with Lucette.

Chapter 42

Thursday, 2nd September 1932

Lucette was taking Odette for her usual walk. They arrived at Aristide and Georgette's house. Both were in the garden. Georgette was tending to the pots of geraniums her English neighbours had entrusted to her when they left after their summer holidays in the house next door. She took pride each year in keeping the flowers alive throughout the winter in order to return them the following spring on their return at Easter.

Aristide was sitting in the shade of the lean-to beside the house where he kept his tools. He was sharpening his knives on the grind-stone and didn't hear Lucette as she came into the garden.

"Lucette!" exclaimed Georgette, seeing her approach. "Come in. It's lovely to see you, and Odette too. Come and sit in the shade. I'll bring out an apéritif and we can have a good chat."

Turning to the little girl, she asked:

"Would you like some juice, Odette?"

She hurried into the house to fetch some biscuits and a bottle of chilled Loupiac. When she returned and sat beside Lucette, Odette was already playing with 'Grandpa' Aristide.

"So, what's new?" she asked, after serving the wine. "You look sad. What's happened, Lucette? Tell me."

"I don't know how to tell you. It's about Marie."

"Marie? It's so long since she left. They're coming back soon, I think. I can't wait to see her."

Lucette gently took her hand.

"That's just it, Georgette. You won't see her. She passed away."

"Dear God! But how? It's not possible ..."

"A violent fever spread through Québec in July and Marie became gravely ill. She died in August."

"But that's so unfair, Lucette! Just when she could have returned having been proved innocent. I'm devastated. It's so sad. The poor young woman. She didn't have an easy life."

"The saddest thing is that we will never know if she knew the whole dreadful business was over and the jewels had been found. She was already in a coma when Alain gave her the news. If she did hear the news hen the relief may have been too much for her."

"That's so sad," said Georgette. "Is Alain still coming back?"

"Yes, he'll be here with their daughter in two weeks time."

"I know it's terrible, but I've forgotten the little one's name."

"Mariette, little Marie."

Printed in Poland
by Amazon Fulfillment
Poland Sp. z o.o., Wrocław

54656282R00123